THE SILENCE

BROKEN AEGIS

DAVID ADAMS

Copyright © 2025 David Adams All rights reserved.
Contact: djadamsbooks@gmail.com

This is a work of fiction. Names, characters, places, and incidents are products of the author's imagination or used fictitiously. Any resemblance to actual persons, living or dead, events, or locales is entirely coincidental.

No part of this book may be reproduced, stored in a retrieval system, or transmitted by any means without the written permission of the author, except for brief quotations used in reviews or scholarly works.

"They begged for light, and I came bearing truth. Now they claw at the dark, wishing they had stayed blind."
— Caelomin

Contents

1. The Feast of the Fallen
2. The Caged Devil
3. The Stranger by the fire
4. Marks in the Firelight
5. Echoes and Invitations
6. Smoke, Splinters, and Strategy
7. Bargain in the Dark
8. The Faith That Binds
9. When the March Began
10. The Unveiling
11. Ashes and Echoes
12. The Blooded Feather
13. Judgment's Edge
14. Ritual and Ruin
15. The Name That Burns
16. The Silence-Broken Aegis

A Note to the Reader

About the author

1

The Feast of the Fallen

The battlefield was silent now, save for the wet squelch of blood-soaked earth beneath armoured boots. Smoke drifted low over the torn land like a mourning veil, and the air stank of iron, fire, and rot. Broken banners fluttered weakly in the dying wind, their colours dulled by ash and gore. Around the scattered corpses of knights and foot soldiers alike, only four knights remained. The survivors stood motionless, eyes hollow, swords slack in their hands. They had lived through the slaughter, but something in the stillness felt *wrong*.

Sir Aldric, the oldest among them, stepped carefully among the fallen on the battlefield, checking for signs of life beneath shattered helms and twisted limbs. His shoulders were heavy with years and grief, his voice long since swallowed by the dead. His eyes lingered on each face, each one a haunting reminder of the path that had led him here. His gaze settled on a young knight who lay motionless on the ground. Kneeling beside him, Aldric checked for any sign of life, and in that fleeting moment, he saw the face of his own son imposed on the fallen knight.

His only son, the one who had defied his father and left for the First Crusade and never returned. The memory washed over him, his son who ran to free the holy land and met his end too soon.

That memory, that regret, was the reason Aldric found himself on yet another battlefield, determined that no other father would have to suffer the same loss.

He bent to lift the body, stared for a long moment, then let it drop without a word.

Near the dying fire, the youngest knight sat hunched, trembling. His name was Corwin. In his bloodied hands he clutched a torn scrap of white fabric, soft and clean despite the filth around him. It was from his betrothed, sent with him for luck. Now it was all he had left that wasn't stained with blood.

Off to one side, a tall figure loomed in the shadows, his armor dented and streaked with gore. This was Sir Garran. Rage boiled in him with no enemy left to face. He swung his sword down again and again on the ruined body of a fallen foe, even though the man had long since stopped breathing. Each strike rang out sharp and hollow across the field.

The last knight, Sir Thomelin, stood apart from the others, his face pale beneath the crust of dirt and dried blood. He moved closer to the fire.

Sir Aldric rose slowly from the last corpse, wiping blood from his gauntlet with a ragged breath. He glanced toward the others, his voice low and rasped with age.

"We're exposed out here," he muttered. "Too exposed. Thomelin, how far are we from the nearest crossing? Or from aid?"

Thomelin didn't look up right away. He stood near the fire looking past the battlefield, eyes scanning the smoke-thick horizon.

"Two days' ride to the nearest stronghold. Reinforcements won't arrive until at least tomorrow, if they come at all."

Aldric swore under his breath, barely more than a sigh. "Then we need to move. We can't stay here among the dead."

Before Thomelin could answer, a steel helm clattered against the stones at their feet. It belonged to one of the fallen.

Sir Garran stood a few paces away, jaw clenched, blood smearing the side of his face. "You're not in charge here, old crow. You might have a few winters on us, but age don't make you a commander."

Aldric turned slowly, meeting his gaze without blinking. But he didn't reply.

"Enough," Thomelin cut in, his voice tense, but not sharp. "We're alone out here. What if the enemy returns in force?"

He pointed across the field, toward the horizon, where dark clouds loomed over the distant hills: heavy, swollen with rain. The treetops swayed beneath them like they, too, sensed what was coming.

"Look at that," Corwin said. "There's a storm coming. We can't stay out in the open."

Thomelin nodded once, rubbing the stubble on his chin. "There's an old watchtower up the ridge. I saw it before the fighting started. Stone's mostly intact, from the look of it."

The tower loomed against the storm like a dying sentinel, its stone pitted and veined with moss. Time had gnawed its corners smooth, but traces of its former life still lingered. Just above the warped wooden door, half-buried in shadow, a carved stone cross hung askew: chipped, rainworn, and nearly swallowed by ivy.

Aldric turned to him. "Then that's where we go. Move fast. Stay alert."

Garran snorted, not bothering to hide the scorn in his voice. "Fine. But don't think you are in charge, Aldric."

He slung his bloodied sword over his shoulder like a butcher's cleaver and started walking toward the ridge.

Thomelin stared into the dark beyond the edge of the firelight and froze. There, carried on the shifting smoke, came a sound. Faint, distant. A low, wet dragging, like something heavy being pulled across the ground.

Night had fallen like a shroud, hiding the broken dead beneath folds of shadow and smoke. The fire from their torches sputtered weakly, casting flickers of orange against dented steel and blood-slicked faces. No one spoke. Words had died with their comrades. Around them, the air was thick, heavy with the reek of scorched flesh and the copper sting of blood.

Then came the sound again, closer this time.

Something was still alive out there.

In the silence, a sound slithered in: a low, wet growl, dragging through the dark like breath through teeth. Something moved among the corpses.

Sir Aldric was the first to rise. His sword slid from its scabbard with a sound like a whisper cut short. He peered into the haze, eyes narrowed, shoulders stiff. The air smelled worse now, like meat left too long in the sun.

Sir Thomelin stood beside him, slower, more deliberate. "That's not the wind," he said.

From the edge of the firelight, Corwin flinched. "It sounds like... something's eating."

A pause. Then a sickening wet *rip*.

Corwin retched, doubling over with one hand on his knee, the other still clutching the torn white scrap of fabric. "God in Heaven..."

Sir Garran's face twisted into fury. He stepped forward with sword already raised, rage masking the fear in his eyes. "We left no wounded. Nothing should be moving."

Aldric held up a hand. "Wait."

They all listened. Another chew, slow and lazy. Something big, shifting weight across the dead like a dog wading through carrion. Bone cracked. There was a crunch of mail, then another wet swallow.

"Do you hear it?" Thomelin said, breath tight.

The fire behind them hissed in the damp. The shadows just beyond the bodies pulsed faintly, like something breathing in the dark.

Drawn by instinct or dread, they rose slowly, as if the weight of their own bones resisted. Torches were lit with trembling hands, the flames catching in the wind, casting wild shadows across the carnage. The moon hung low and bruised behind the smoke, offering only a sickly light as they stepped over corpses bloated in their armor. The growling came again, louder now, wet and rhythmic, like meat torn from bone. The men moved as one, blades half-raised, breath held. Then they saw it. A shape hunched low in the mire, darker than the night itself. Its limbs were too long, its back arched like a beast, and it tore at the dead with a hunger not born of nature. Flesh peeled under its claws, and bone cracked between its jaws.

They crouched behind the ruin of a shattered cart, the firelight behind them barely reaching this far. From their hiding place, they watched the thing feed. It moved with a savage rhythm: ripping, tearing, slurping at blood like a starving hound. Its skin, or what passed for it, was black and slick, glinting like wet stone in the moonlight. It was human-sized, but nothing human remained in its form. No prayers came to their lips. The Church had spoken of salvation, of glory in battle, but never of this. This was not a test of faith. This was a nightmare dragged from hell.

Corwin crouched lower behind the cart, his knuckles white around the hilt of his sword. His voice was barely more than a breath.

"What kind of monster is that?" he asked.

No one answered at first. Only the wet sounds of feeding filled the space between them. The thing had torn open a corpse's ribcage and was rooting through the organs like a boar through soil.

Sir Garran spat, "Doesn't matter what it is. It eats our dead. That's reason enough to kill it."

Sir Aldric frowned, watching the creature's movements closely. "It's strong. Look at the size of it. Those limbs... that weight. It's too big and moving too fast. One wrong move and it could tear through us."

Thomelin whispered, "We might not survive a straight fight in the open."

The thing stopped feeding for a moment, lifting its head as though listening. Its face (or what passed for one) was smeared in blood. No eyes were visible. Just slits, ridges, and a maw lined with fangs too long for any natural skull.

"God save us," Corwin murmured. "That thing's not of this world."

Aldric's gaze narrowed. "If we fight it head-on, one of us dies. Maybe all of us."

"It's distracted," Thomelin said, his mind turning quickly, voice sharper now. "It's gorged. Slower, maybe weaker. If we can lure it..."

"To where?" Garran snapped.

Thomelin turned to him. "The old watchtower. The bottom level has a storage chamber room: low ceilings, thick stone, iron bars cage on the far wall. I saw them when I scouted past it. Looked like it was once used as a prison or kennel."

Garran scowled. "You want to trap *that* in a dusty old room?"

"If the cage holds, yes," Thomelin said. "We don't need to kill it, just lock it away."

"And if it breaks free?"

"Then it does it behind stone, not in the open with our backs turned."

Aldric considered it, eyes never leaving the creature. It had returned to feeding now, gorging as though the dead were a feast laid in offering.

He nodded once. "We lure it. Trap it. Then pray the cage holds."

Corwin's hand trembled as he wiped sweat from his brow. "How do we get it to follow us?"

The others hesitated, staring back at the beast, still feasting. They felt no courage, only the raw instinct to flee. But the creature was close to the tower. Close enough, maybe. One of the bodies near it still wore a battered surcoat: red, like fresh blood. An idea formed. They could bait it. Lure it with more flesh. Or worse... with one of their own.

2

The Caged Devil

Thomelin's voice was cold and certain. "We show it something living."

The four of them crouched behind the wreckage, the stench of death thick around them, their breaths shallow. The creature was still feeding, still lost in its obscene banquet... but for how long, none of them could say.

Sir Thomelin looked to Aldric. "We can make it work. But each of us must play a part."

Aldric nodded. "Quick and precise. Garran, circle wide. Use the smoke and the hill's cover. Get to the tower and open the outer door. Make sure the path to the storage room is clear."

Garran grunted in assent. "If I see you're dead when I get back, I'm sealing the damn door and taking the high road myself."

Thomelin smirked without humor. "Noted."

Aldric turned to Corwin. The boy looked pale, his lips trembling, but he met the old knight's eyes. The white scrap of fabric still clung to his fingers.

"You'll be the bait." Corwin was young, quick on his feet, and most importantly, not yet broken like the rest.

Corwin's throat bobbed. "I thought as much."

"We'll keep eyes on you the whole time," Aldric said. "You just need to run. Lead it through the arch, into the tower's storage room. Once it enters the storage room, you go right of the cage. Thomelin will be waiting at the cage's iron gate to slam it shut."

Corwin nodded slowly, his fingers tightening around the fabric. "And if I trip?"

"Then scream," Garran said. "We'll know what to do. I'd prefer a straight fight anyway."

Thomelin looked to Aldric. "You'll need to get its attention. Pull it from the feeding. Loudly."

Aldric glanced down at the rusted spear beside one of the corpses. "I'll manage."

"Then let's move," Thomelin said, rising.

The plan was madness. But madness was all they had left.

The others lay in wait. The trap was simple but brutal: draw it in, slam the cage shut, bolt the iron bar. Corwin would slip out the side once the thing entered. At least, that was the hope.

Behind them, the Bishop's promise rang like prophecy in their minds: gold beyond measure. Forgiveness eternal. A place at God's right hand. What better proof of divine power than delivering unto the Church a living devil? Plus they had been told they were God's chosen, God is with them.

Sir Garran and Corwin slipped away into the fog and smoke, Garran's broad form vanishing into the gloom like a predator on the prowl. Every footstep was deliberate, careful, armor shifting with the barest whisper. They moved in unison, keeping low, keeping to the broken shapes of fallen men, the splintered carts, the scattered shields half-sunken in mud.

The beast was still feeding. Still tearing. But slower now, its grotesque meal half-devoured. Its limbs twitched occasionally, as if readying for something. As Garran crept up the slope toward the tower, the thing stopped mid-bite.

It lifted its head.

The knights froze.

For a heartbeat, the battlefield seemed to hold its breath.

It turned... slowly, impossibly... and faced the tower. Its body hunched lower, as though sniffing the air. Garran and Corwin dropped flat behind shattered debris.

Thomelin's whisper barely reached Aldric through the smoke: "It knows."

Aldric's hand tightened around the rusted spear.

"No," he muttered, more to himself than the others. "No, not yet."

He stepped out from cover and hurled the spear with all his strength. It spun in a perfect arc through the air and struck the creature clean across the shoulder.

Clang.

The spear bounced harmlessly off its slick, black hide. Not even a stagger.

The beast turned.

Not toward Garran and Corwin, but toward *them*.

Corwin stepped out and began shouting, raw and desperate, echoing across the field. "Come! Demon! Come taste the blood of the living!"

Its face (if such a thing could be called a face) twisted. There was no rage in it. Only hunger.

Garran's blood ran cold. "Run, boy."

Corwin didn't need to be told twice. He broke into a sprint, lungs already burning, heart slamming against his ribs. Behind him, the creature let out a sound... part growl, part roar, part *something else*. Something unnatural. It lunged forward like a battering ram of sinew and claw.

Garran, watching from the far end near the tower, gritted his teeth. "Saints preserve him..."

The ground was slick and treacherous. Corwin stumbled but kept his feet. The tower loomed ahead, its broken door already hanging open. Garran had done his part.

Closer.

He could hear it behind him now, the slap of wet limbs in the mud, the dragging scrape of claws. A harsh breath like steam through stone.

Closer.

He reached the tower steps in full sprint. He didn't slow. Inside: dark. Cold. The stink of mold and rot. He hurtled toward the storage room at the rear, the cage's iron frame just visible in the gloom beyond.

The beast's claw scraped the stone just behind him.

Too close.

Corwin screamed and grabbed the edge of the open cage door, *spun with it*, using the momentum to pivot and veer hard left. His boots skidded on the floor. The beast had no time to adjust. It slammed into the cage at full speed, headfirst, howling as iron bars folded around it.

"NOW!"

Thomelin stepped from the shadows and *slammed* the cage door shut.

The lock clanged. The bolt dropped. The sound was like a funeral bell.

For a moment... silence.

Then the beast shrieked.

It wasn't the cry of pain. It was *violation*. Fury. Horror. A roar torn from a throat not built for any human sound. It shook the iron so hard the hinges screamed. The entire frame of the cage rattled as it flung itself again and again into the bars, eyes gleaming with red-black hate.

Sir Aldric was already pulling Corwin out by the collar. "Out... now, move!"

Thomelin slammed the storage room door behind them as the cage inside groaned again under another blow. The latch dropped into place. Garran shoved a rusted beam through the brackets.

They stepped back, panting, as the door thudded once... twice... from within.

Then silence.

Or something like it.

Only the storm still spoke outside.

Aldric exhaled slowly. "Saints forgive us... we caught it."

Corwin collapsed to his knees, trembling, blood and rain soaking his face.

And from within the storage room, muffled by stone and wood, came the slow, dragging sound of something *waiting*.

The wind clawed at the tower as they sealed the heavy wooden door behind them. Rain had begun to fall in thick, icy drops, hissing against the stone like whispers. The fire they'd built sputtered in the hearth pit at the center of the main room, casting a flickering amber glow that did little to banish the shadows lurking in the corners.

The tower itself was old, far older than it looked from the ridge. Built first as a chapel in centuries past, its foundation bore the bones of forgotten prayer. The rounded arches still bore faint traces of worn carvings: saints with faceless visages, angels with broken wings. At some point, perhaps during another war, it had been repurposed into a watchtower. The altar had long since been torn away, replaced with stone benches and racks for weapons that were now empty.

Thin arrow-slit windows punctured the walls like wounds, overlooking the battlefield below. Through them, the knights could see the sea of corpses laid out beneath the storm clouds: an ocean of steel and flesh gone still. Smoke from smoldering siege engines rose like incense in a blasphemous mass.

The main chamber had only two points of note: the hearth, and the storage room door.

It stood at the rear of the chamber, thick and bolted, with a small square window at eye level, covered by a rusted iron grate. Beyond it was only darkness now. And the faint, unnatural sound of breathing.

Sir Garran sat on an overturned crate, his sword across his knees, eyes locked on the storage door like it might lunge from the wall at any moment.

Corwin huddled closer to the fire, still shaking despite the heat. His face was pale, and the scrap of white cloth hung limp in his hand, forgotten for now.

Sir Thomelin stood by one of the arrow slits, his gaze fixed on the battlefield outside, though his mind was clearly elsewhere.

Sir Aldric remained on his feet, his arms folded, eyes sunken deep in thought.

It was Garran who broke the silence. "What in God's name is it?"

No one answered at first.

Thomelin spoke without looking away from the door. "It moved like no beast I've ever seen. Too fast for its size."

Corwin swallowed. "And the way it looked at me. Like it *knew*. Not like an animal. Like something that could *choose*."

Aldric rubbed his jaw, the scruff there slick with rain and grime. "It's not natural. That much is clear."

"An unholy abomination," Thomelin muttered. "A demon. Or worse."

Corwin glanced toward the storage room door. "Can the cage hold it?"

Another silence.

Aldric looked toward the door. The wood shook faintly, as though the thing inside shifted its weight or brushed against the bars.

He spoke at last, his voice low. "I don't know."

Garran finally looked up. "Then we should finish it now. Fire. Blade. Whatever it takes."

"We don't know *how* to kill it. That spear bounced off it," Thomelin replied. "And if we fail, it gets loose again."

Aldric's gaze lingered on the arrow-slit window beside him, watching the rain blur the battlefield. "The storm's almost here. And we need rest. Scattered. Reinforcements were supposed to arrive before nightfall. If they haven't, they'll come with the dawn."

He turned back to them.

"We wait. Keep watch. Seal the door if we must. But no one opens that room. Not until help arrives."

Corwin nodded faintly, drawing his knees up to his chest.

Garran didn't answer. He simply resumed sharpening his sword with slow, deliberate strokes.

Outside, thunder rumbled in the distance... long and low, like the groaning of something vast awakening beneath the earth.

From behind the storage door, the sound came again. Breathing. But slower now. Rhythmic. As though it were *listening*.

3

The Stranger by the fire

The rain came suddenly, thick and cold, lashing sideways as the storm swept over the battlefield like a curse. Thunder cracked across the heavens, and what few fires still burned outside hissed into steam. The four men stood just inside the tower's entrance, cold and shivering, eyes drifting toward the storage room with the cage and the beast.

"Can we... can we spend the night in the tower with that thing?" Corwin asked, barely above a whisper.

No one answered.

Sir Aldric rose without a word, the weight of years and battle hanging heavy on his frame. The firelight danced across his armor as he crossed the stone floor, each step measured, cautious. The others watched but said nothing. He stopped before the storage room door, its iron latch cold beneath his fingers. Leaning in, he peered through the small barred window. Inside, the room was cloaked in shadow, the faint flicker of firelight from the main chamber barely reaching the cage beyond. He could just make it out: the silhouette of iron, twisted slightly where the beast had struck it.

The creature sat motionless in the cage, limbs folded in a way no man could imitate. Its skin glistened black beneath the light shining through, slick with blood and rainwater. But it wasn't its form that unnerved them most. It was its stare. It didn't look confused or panicked. It looked calm. *Amused.*

"I don't like how it's looking at us," Aldric said. "There's something in its eyes. Like it *knows* us. Like it's already won." He hesitated. "It's smiling. Not with its mouth... with its *eyes*."

A silence fell over them, broken only by the storm hammering at the tower walls.

"Maybe it's exactly where it wants to be," Thomelin muttered.

"Let it smile in the dark," Aldric whispered as he put a wooden beam across the outside of the door.

But even after the room was sealed, they still felt its gaze. Like it had seeped into the walls. Like the storm outside had brought more than rain.

The fire crackled and popped, its feeble warmth doing little against the creeping cold that seeped through the cracked stones of the tower. Shadows danced madly on the walls, rising and falling like ghosts trying to claw their way free. The men sat in silence, the flickering light painting their faces with hollow eyes and sunken cheeks.

The window in the old storage room door was no wider than a fist, but they all stared at it as if it were the mouth of Hell itself. Something moved beyond it now and then: quiet, subtle, a breath or scrape just enough to remind them they were not alone.

The storm battered the tower with relentless fury. Wind screamed through shattered slits in the stone, and rain lashed against what remained of the wooden shutters. It was as if the heavens themselves wanted the place washed away.

"When can we expect the others to get here?" Corwin asked, his voice barely louder than a whisper, as if to speak too loudly might wake something.

"Not till at least tomorrow now with that storm," came the reply.

A pause.

"Any chance of locals coming back?"

Aldric, who was now wrapped in a thick, tattered cloak he found, leaned forward. His eyes had not left the hole in the door since they'd lit the fire. When he spoke, his voice was dry as parchment, but steady.

"I'm more concerned about the beast in the cage," he said. "It's not natural."

No one answered.

Thunder rolled above, shaking loose dust from the rafters. The flames jumped. From behind the door, a low sound came: wet, guttural. Not quite a growl. Not quite a voice.

The men looked at each other, fear plain in their eyes. They didn't bother to hide it anymore.

"Was that the beast that made the noise?" Corwin asked, barely breathing the words.

"Don't be daft," snapped Garran, though his voice cracked. "It's a beast. Nothing more."

But before the lie could settle in the room, a sound came from the next chamber: soft at first, then heavier. Something shifting. A dragging noise. A scrape like nails on stone.

"Can it get out of that cage?"

"No," came the reply, sharp and rehearsed. "Solid iron. It's locked. And the storage door's barred. That beam's thick as a man's thigh."

Still, no one looked away from the door. The fire seemed smaller now, the shadows bolder.

"We should get some rest."

Then BANG.

A violent knock at the main door behind them.

The men jumped, several reaching for swords or whatever weapons they had close at hand. The tower groaned under the storm's weight, and the flames danced higher, startled by the sudden gust of panic.

Another BANG, followed by a voice, muffled by rain and wood.

"Open the door! Please! Let me in!"

A man's voice. Desperate. Cold.

No one moved.

The banging came again. Louder. Faster. A fist... no, fists. Maybe more than one. Pounding.

"Could be one of ours," Garran said, half rising.

"Could be a trap," muttered Aldric.

From the storage room, another sound answered. A low chuff. A rattling chain.

The men approached the main door, blades half-drawn, eyes wary.

"Speak: friend or foe," Aldric called out, his voice firm despite the trembling in his hand.

From beyond the thick wooden door came the reply: "Please... it's cold, and wet. My group was ambushed. They're all dead. I saw our banner above the tower. I serve the same Lord as you. I fight for the bishop... and for God."

The wind screamed behind him, as if protesting.

A sharp, metallic *clang* from the storage room snapped every head around. Chains rattled. Something shifted, heavier this time.

"Let him in," Corwin said quickly, panic licking at the edge of his voice.

They pulled the bolt free. The door creaked open with effort, the storm immediately flooding the room with rain and the roar of the wind. A figure stepped in, hunched, cloaked, soaked through. Mud clung to his boots. The firelight caught the colors beneath his cloak: *their* colors. The crest of their lord, tattered but unmistakable.

But something was off. His posture too still. His face hidden. And though he said nothing more, the air around him seemed heavier, colder somehow.

He moved to the fire without a word, knelt close to it. Steam curled from his soaked clothes. The door was bolted again behind him. The room seemed to grow smaller.

"Should we tell him?" one of the men whispered.

"Tell me what?" he asked, not looking up.

His voice was calm. Too calm. As if he already knew.

The fire snapped again. The door to the storage room let out a long, low creak: wood strained against something pushing from the other side.

The newcomer did not flinch.

The newcomer sat motionless, his hands outstretched toward the fire, fingers long and still. His face remained hidden beneath the hood, but every so often, a flicker of flame caught his cheek, casting fleeting shapes across pale skin.

"We caught a devil beast," the youngest knight said, his voice trying to sound braver than it was.

The newcomer didn't move. Then, softly, "Yet none of you seem wounded from his capture. Don't you think it was a bit too easy... catching him?"

A pause.

"What if he *wanted* you to think that you had caught him?"

Silence followed, then a sharp glance from the old knight.

"Him?" he said, narrowing his eyes.

Another stirring from the next room. A low scrape. A shuffle of weight against stone. The knights flinched again, all turning to the iron-banded door with its narrow hole: watching, waiting.

All except the oldest knight, who hadn't once taken his eyes off the man at the fire.

The newcomer slowly turned his head toward the sealed door. "Why do you think it's a beast?"

The youngest stepped forward, voice cracking with heat. "It was feeding. On the flesh of the fallen. It drank blood like wine." He pointed to the door, jaw clenched. "We trapped it. For the bishop. To cast it back into hell."

The man stood. Slowly. Deliberately.

The other knights tensed. Hands drifted toward hilts. Armor creaked.

Without a word, the stranger walked across the room, boots echoing softly on the stone. He stopped before the door, before the tiny hole. He leaned forward and peered through it, his back to them now, still as stone.

The fire cracked behind him. The rain lashed the tower walls. Wind moaned through unseen cracks. And then, only silence.

Then he spoke, so low they barely heard him:

"You should let it go free... while you still can."

The stranger leaned toward the barred window, muttering softly in a voice too old for his body: words the knights didn't recognize, but felt.

He didn't turn. Just stared into the dark.

"You think that old iron will hold? That door was made for men, not for *him*."

His voice deepened, cracking at the edges.

"The cage buys time. Nothing more."

A pause.

"When the darkness comes again, and it will, you'll wish you'd run. Or died."

"You've locked yourselves in with him... not the other way around."

Behind the door, the metal cage stirred. Something breathed.

The newcomer didn't turn. His voice came low, almost lost in the sound of the rain against stone.

"I've heard of creatures like this," he said. "They change shape. Feast on flesh. They can crawl into your thoughts, twist your senses. Make you see things that aren't there. Hear things that never were. It will poison you."

A pause.

"None of you will survive this night."

The youngest knight took a step back, his breath hitching.

Thomelin spoke up, desperate, defiant. "It's locked in a cage. In a locked room. We are chosen by God to do His work. God *will* protect us."

As if in response, thunder cracked louder than before. A blast of wind slammed into the tower, and the heavy outside door blasted open with a shriek. Rain and cold burst in, and the fire nearly died, shrinking to a shivering core of embers.

The room dimmed in an instant. Shadows swallowed the walls.

"Shut the door!" someone shouted.

They moved in a panic, slamming the door shut again, struggling to get the bolt across. One knight knelt by the fire, shielding it from the wind as another lit a torch with shaking hands. The flames sputtered, then caught, casting erratic light across the stone.

And then someone said it, quietly, but with growing fear:

"Where is he?"

They turned.

The newcomer was gone.

4

Marks in the Firelight

The firelight danced wildly across empty stone. No sound. No trace. No footprints on the wet floor. No creak of door or steps.

"Where did he go?" the young knight asked, voice high with tension.

The others looked around the cramped space. There wasn't much room in the tower. No closets, no chambers above. Just the main hall, the storage room... and the cage.

"There's nowhere to hide," one said. "Not in here."

"Was he even real?" Corwin whispered. "Was he some kind of trick... something the beast made us see?"

A heavy silence fell.

Then, from behind the storage room door, came a noise.

Not the scrape from before. Not the chain's rattle.

But a *laugh*.

Low. Quiet. Not forced. Not human.

A soft, dark chuckle that echoed through the cracks in the stone, dragging behind it a sense of something *watching*.

The youngest knight took a step back from the door.

Inside the cage, the thing moved.

The knights stood in a tight circle, blades half-drawn, faces pale in the flickering torchlight. The fire had returned to life, but its warmth didn't reach them. It just cast long, shaking shadows.

"We need to check the storage room," one of them muttered. "Make sure... make sure that thing is still in the cage. And that the stranger, if he's real, ain't in there with it."

No one moved.

"I heard it... moving," Thomelin added.

A pause.

Then *a voice.*

Not loud. Not angry.

Soft. Measured. Gentle.

It came from behind the storage room door.

"You should have let him out."

The youngest knight went stiff. "That's... that's the stranger."

"No," the old knight whispered, eyes locked on the sealed door. "No, it's not."

It was the same voice... *almost.* But something was wrong with it now. It dragged in the throat, deeper, slicker. There was a subtle growl under the syllables, a rasp like wind through bone.

The torchlight dimmed slightly, the flames bowing as though to something unseen.

The men looked at each other. No one breathed.

The knights crept closer to the door, steel drawn, the fire's glow clinging to their backs like the last warmth of life.

Thomelin stepped forward, hand trembling on his hilt.

"Speak, demon! We are God's chosen. You will *obey* me!"

Silence.

Only the whisper of the wind through the cracks. The faint hiss of the fire behind them.

Aldric moved beside the door and squinted through the hole. "Can't see in," he muttered. "Too dark."

"Throw in a torch."

One of them nodded, pulled a smaller torch from the fire, and flung it through the narrow gap as they unbarred the storage room door just enough to slip it through. It landed with a sputtering bounce, rolling halfway into the chamber before settling on its side.

Its flame licked the floor, casting a half-circle of light across the stone. They all leaned in.

No sign of the stranger and the cage... empty.

A beat of stunned silence.

But just beyond the torchlight, squatting in the corner, still as death, was a figure. Black and hunched. Limbs too long, too crooked. The firelight didn't quite reach it, but it was there.

Watching.

Waiting.

Aldric turned to the others, his voice low and grim.

"It got out the cage."

Aldric closed and bolted the storage room door hastily.

A choked breath escaped Corwin. "How did it get out? The cage is solid iron. Bolted."

The old knight stepped forward, his holy cross now in one hand, sword gripped tight in the other. He looked in the window gap.

"Is this another trick, demon?" he growled. "Speak!"

The shadow didn't move.

Then, it did.

A slow, fluid tilt of the head. Not toward the door, but *up,* as if smelling something in the air.

Then the voice returned, richer now, deeper. No longer just inside the room. It seemed to *creep* under the door, curl into their ears.

"You wear the cross like armor..." it said.

A pause.

"...but does it guard you from truth... or bind you to it?"

The old knight took a step closer to the door, torchlight flickering across the sweat-lined steel of his brow. He held the cross high, letting it catch the firelight.

His voice didn't shake as he declared:

"Truth is the blade I bear, and the cross is my shield. I do not wear it to hide from darkness. I wear it to face it."

A low sound slithered from the dark: half breath, half growl. Then the voice returned, sliding beneath the door like oil through cracks.

"Then tell me, knight...

When that blade breaks... when that shield splinters... and your god does not answer...

Will you still call it truth... or just silence in a different shape?"

It paused, as if savoring the weight of the words.

"Faith is loud in the daylight. I wonder what it sounds like... when you're screaming in the dark."

The old knight lowered his cross, eyes hard as iron. He turned to the others, jaw clenched tight.

"We need to kill it. Now. Before it poisons our minds like it did the air."

The youngest stepped back slightly, his voice trembling beneath the weight of fear.

"What if we can't?"

He glanced toward the sealed door.

"We should wait for the bishop. For the others. He'll know how to destroy this thing... properly."

The old knight's face darkened.

"No." He shook his head once, firmly.

"It must be us. This thing... it's already working on us. Every moment we wait, it digs deeper. We cannot afford to wait."

Garran stepped toward the door, sword low but ready. His voice was steadier, but cautious.

"Whom do you serve, monster?"

Silence.

Only the fire cracking behind them. Only the storm outside, hammering the world.

They waited. Still. Breathless. Listening for any sound: movement, whisper, even breath.

Nothing.

Then a *slow* sound. Something dragging lightly across stone. A finger, perhaps. Or a claw.

Then the voice, calm again. Not loud. But every word felt *close*.

A stillness settled over the room. Not peace... *pressure.* As if the tower itself was holding its breath.

Then the beast spoke again.

Its voice had deepened, scraped raw by something too old for language, too dark for flesh. It didn't shout. It *spoke,* and the stones listened.

"Was it revelation that called you to war...

...or a whisper in the dark, wearing a holy face?"

The knights stood motionless. No answer. Not one dared speak. The fire cracked once, weakly. Rain battered the tower.

Then came the voice again, worse now, fractured at the edges, as if it no longer came from a single throat:

"The blood you spill sings louder than your prayers."

"Whose altar do you think it feeds?"

A slow, dragging breath. Not tired... *savoring*.

"In the first silence, before the stars were named, the lie was spoken: 'I am the only.'"

"Tell me, knight... how many thrones sit in your heaven?"

The youngest knight stepped forward. His lips trembled. His voice shook, barely holding together the fragile armor of belief.

"We... we are the chosen. We serve the One True God."

Silence.

Then the voice returned, and it no longer sounded like it came from the cage.

It sounded like it came from *everywhere*.

"There are no chosen."

A scraping sound behind the walls. Above. Below.

"Only the marked."

The fire dimmed as if recoiling.

"And you...

...are all marked."

The old knight stepped forward, his shadow long against the firelight, cross gripped tightly in one hand, sword in the other. His voice rose: not in panic, but in *conviction,* ringing through the tower like a bell before a funeral.

"Are you afraid of the light?" he called out, eyes fixed on the sealed door.

"Afraid of us? Of God?"

The echo of his words lingered, as if the very walls were weighing them.

For a moment, nothing. Only the storm.

Then... a sound. Not laughter this time.

Breathing. Heavy. Slow. A breath so deep it sounded like it came from the roots of the world.

Then, the voice, now distorted, as if passed through smoke and bone:

"The light?"

It *chuckled*, low and cruel.

"I was there when your sun was lit."

"I watched it stutter into flame... and I laughed then, too."

"Afraid?"

Something *scraped* the inside of the storage room door. Not a hand. A *horn*. Or something harder.

"Not afraid. Just... patient."

"Because I do not need to kill you."

The demon's words hung in the air like smoke that wouldn't rise.

"I only need to watch you lose your God... piece by piece."

The silence that followed wasn't calm. It was *waiting*.

Corwin, the youngest, scratched at his forearm.

"Something's... under my skin," he muttered.

He pulled back the sleeve of his chainmail, revealing bare skin slick with sweat. At first, there was nothing.

Then the torchlight caught it: *a mark*. A twisted symbol, like a spiral carved into flesh, *not made by any blade*.

It pulsed. Once.

The others backed away, eyes wide.

"I didn't... I swear I didn't...!"

Another knight checked his own arm. "There's one on me too," he said hoarsely. "I thought it was a bruise. But it's *moving*."

The old knight didn't look. He already knew.

He turned back to the fire, gripping his cross so hard his knuckles turned white.

But the fire was no longer just fire.

Inside its twisting tongues, *faces* began to form. *Not flames shaped like faces.* Real ones: staring back at him, writhing in pain, reaching. Familiar. His brothers-in-arms. His friends. His *son.*

Each flame whispered his name.

He took a staggering step back.

One of the knights behind him gasped and pointed to the tower door.

Outside, through the cracks, they heard something new.

Voices.

Muffled. Wrong. But... familiar.

5

Echoes and Invitations

"Let us in," came a whisper, broken by the wind.

Another: "Aldric... open the door. I can't feel my legs."

The youngest dropped his torch.

"That's... that's Edran," he whispered. "He died. I saw him die."

The voices came again, clearer now, *more of them.*

Pleading. Crying. *Calling them by name.*

From behind the sealed storage room door, the demon laughed.

The fire hissed low, its flames casting flickering shapes on the walls. Faces still danced in the heat: twisting, burning, calling their names. But something had changed.

Now, they weren't just *faces.*

They were *futures.*

Sir Aldric leaned forward, unable to look away. His mouth opened slightly, breath caught in his throat.

There, within the heart of the fire, he saw *himself.*

Bound in rusted chains. Kneeling before a twisted altar. A hand (not his own) gripping the back of his neck, forcing his head down as something dark and winged loomed above.

He stumbled back, choking.

Thomelin gasped, pointing. "That... That's *me!*" he cried.

His flame showed him impaled, a sword driven through his back, still reaching toward the cross around his neck as blood ran down the stone.

Garran's breath caught as the flames shifted, and in their dancing heart he saw himself: older, the lines of shame carved deep around his eyes. He was on his knees in a circle of broken shields, his sword cast aside, his hands raised in surrender. His voice (a ragged, pleading rasp) spilled from his own mouth as he begged unseen men for mercy. The sight struck him harder than any wound: not a warrior's death, but a small, shivering end without honor. His jaw clenched, and he turned from the fire as if it might brand the image into his skull. He wiped a trembling hand across his mouth, refusing to let the others see the raw horror in his eyes. It was not the pain that shook him.

A voice slid through the dark, soft as old bruises: *"There is no other end for you, Garran. On your knees, begging, forgotten."*

His vision blurred, the image of himself (kneeling, begging) burning behind his eyes. A heat rose in his chest, shame and fury tangled so tight he couldn't breathe. In the crackle of the flames, he heard it: a voice no louder than a thought, but cold and certain. *"That is your truth, Garran. Not a warrior. Not a knight. Just a frightened man waiting for someone else to decide his worth."* His hand went to the hilt of his sword, knuckles white. *"There is no other end for you."* The breath caught in his throat, and something broke: something that had held all his grief and rage in check. He would not let that vision be the last of him. If death waited behind that door, he would meet it on his feet, blade in hand, not crawling in the dark.

One by one, they saw their ends, *except one.*

Corwin, the youngest, stared into the fire... and saw *nothing.*

No flames.

Just darkness.

"I don't see anything," he said, voice small.

The others turned toward him, silent.

No one knew what it meant.

Before they could speak, the whispering outside returned.

But different now.

Angrier.

"You left me," came the first voice: soft, breathy, and broken. "I begged... and you turned away."

Another: "We *bled* for you."

The wind picked up, but the voices rose above it.

"I *trusted* you, Aldric."

The knight spun toward the door. "That's not...! That's not what happened!"

He took a step forward.

Thomelin grabbed his shoulder, hard. "It's not them."

But the voices kept coming.

"You prayed while I burned."

"You hid behind your God."

"You let the beast in."

Aldric's face crumpled, fists clenched at his sides. "Shut up," he whispered. "Shut *up*."

A silence fell, heavy and absolute.

Then, from behind the storage door, the demon spoke again: its voice calm, measured, *smiling*.

"They remember."

"But I forgive you."

Garran began to tremble. His hands clutched at his head, breaths short and ragged.

"I can't... I *can't* take this anymore."

He staggered forward, shoving past the others.

"*Enough!* I won't sit here and wait to die!"

The others, Corwin, was still staring into the fire, mouth parted, eyes glazed. The old knight stood near the tower entrance, whispering hoarsely to the voices in the storm, "Forgive me... I did what I could. Please... not like this..."

Garran lifted the heavy beam and threw the door wide. Darkness greeted him.

And something *waiting* in it.

He raised his blade and charged inside, shouting a war cry that twisted into a scream halfway through.

Then *SLAM!*

The door crashed shut behind him on its own, with a force that shook the tower. The beam dropped across it again, *without any of them touching it.*

A cold wind rushed through the chamber, extinguishing one of the torches.

Then came the sounds.

Screaming.

Flesh tearing.

Bones snapping like dry branches.

Each cry from inside was worse than the last: growing thinner, shorter, until only a wet crunch remained.

The other knights snapped from their trances.

Corwin turned, wide-eyed. "*Who went in?!*"

They rushed to the storage room door. The old knight peered in the caged window.

The flickering torch inside still burned where it had landed earlier. Its dim glow lit part of the chamber.

A body lay in the center of the floor.

Their companion, slumped, bloodied, unmoving. Limbs twisted unnaturally. A halo of blood spread beneath him like a dark sun.

Corwin gripped the door. "We must help him! We can't just leave him!"

The old knight didn't move. His voice was low. Cold.

"It's too late."

He stepped back from the door, eyes hollow.

"He's already gone."

A long, still moment followed. The only sound was the wind clawing at the tower walls.

Then, softly, but clear, the demon spoke again.

"He is still alive..."

A pause.

"...because I *want* that."

The words slid through the cracks like smoke, curling into their ears, leaving something cold behind.

Corwin's eyes widened. "Then we can still get him. We can still *save* him."

He moved toward the door, but Aldric caught his arm, grip iron-strong.

"No," the old knight growled. "It's a trap. It's *toying* with us. Keeping him alive just long enough to draw us in."

"But he's still breathing..."

"Because it *wants* you to go in after him." Aldric's voice cracked like dry wood. "That's the game. You'll die before you reach him, and your screams will join his."

Corwin yanked his arm free, chest heaving, torn between courage and fear. But he didn't move.

Sir Thomelin stepped forward, slowly, his gaze locked on the storage door.

His voice was calm, but sharp as a blade in the dark.

"You speak in riddles, monster. You twist faith, wear pain like a crown... But tell me this..."

He took one step closer.

"*What God do you bow down to?*"

Silence.

Thick. Drenched in anticipation.

The question hung in the air, sharp as steel.

For a heartbeat, nothing answered.

Then, from behind the sealed door, came a sound. Not laughter exactly. Something wetter. Thicker. A *smiling noise* made with meat instead of joy.

When the voice came, it was slow... almost tender.

"God..."

A soft exhale, like breath over bone.

"I remember when that word meant something."

The flames bent low.

"I remember the first time it was whispered by broken men, staring up at the dark, begging for someone to answer."

A pause. Wet lips forming a grin they could not see.

"But nothing came."

A creak of iron from within the storage room.

"So they made their own gods. Gave them names. Built them crowns of bone and gold. Swore they could hear them whisper in the wind."

Another silence.

Then the voice returned, closer now, though the door never moved.

"I was there when the first altar was raised... not to *worship*..."

A breath.

"...but to *beg*."

The fire popped.

The next words came soft, slow, crawling through the stone:

"I remember the gods...

I remember the *sound* they made...

...when they died."

The knights stood frozen, the firelight now dim and cold as if recoiling from what it had just heard.

Sir Aldric's mouth moved, but no words came. His sword dipped an inch, the weight of age (or truth) dragging it low.

Corwin clutched the scrap of white fabric tighter in his hand, knuckles bone-white. His lips trembled, eyes wide.

Then the demon spoke again: soft and close, as though whispering directly into his ear.

"Little knight..."

Corwin flinched.

"...you still carry her gift, don't you?"

The fabric in his hand burned cold.

"So clean. So *pure*. Like you thought bringing it would keep her safe... or keep *you* good."

The voice curved like a blade through his thoughts.

"Do you think she waits for you still? Prays for your return? Or has she moved on... like skin from bone?"

Corwin made a choked sound, shaking his head.

"You dream of her at night, don't you? Her hair. Her touch. But when the dreams turn dark, she will be the first person I kill when I leave here. I'll wear her dead face."

"Stop," Corwin whispered. "Please..."

Sir Thomelin stepped forward, planting himself between Corwin and the door, his frame cutting the firelight like a blade.

"That's enough," he said, voice steady. "You feed on fear, but let's test your pride."

He took a step closer, eyes fixed on the narrow hole in the storage door.

"If you are so wise... so powerful... if you've outlived gods and watched them die..."

He narrowed his eyes.

"...then why are you in *our* cage? Why are you behind *our* door?"

Silence.

Then a slow scraping sound. A claw over stone? Or just something pretending to be?

The voice came again: unshaken, but colder now.

"You think you caged me?"

It chuckled: a low, wet rattle that echoed like something caught between a breath and a death rattle.

Then, the voice returned, coiled, intimate, thick with something close to amusement.

"You speak of locks... of doors..."

A drag of something (metal or bone) across stone.

"Do you truly believe that iron bars and old wood keep *me* here?"

The fire dimmed slightly.

"I could leave... *if* I wished."

A pause.

"Perhaps I already have."

Something shifted behind the door. A soft scrape. A stillness that felt wrong.

"But sometimes, knight... sometimes it's not the bars that bind. Sometimes..."

Another breath. Not air, just sound.

"...a cage is just a place you choose to *wait*."

A silence followed, long and terrible.

Sir Thomelin's brow furrowed.

He glanced at the door: not at the bolts, but at the stones around it. The floor beneath. The arch above.

Then he looked back at the others.

And for the first time, he said what none of them wanted to voice:

"I don't think it can get out."

The others turned toward him, startled.

"But I think... *it doesn't want us to know that.*"

Silence.

Then a *sound.*

Not a word.

Not a scream.

A *groan*: wet and guttural, like molten stone churning beneath a ruined altar. It rose from behind the door, rattling the bones of the tower itself.

The fire *surged*, flames stretching unnaturally tall, flaring white, then snapping low as if slapped by an unseen hand.

The ground quivered. The walls creaked. Dust rained down from the ceiling like ash shaken loose from an old, angry god.

The knights flinched back.

The storage room door pulsed outward once, just a breath, then settled.

Then came stillness.

A heavy, bruised silence, as if the tower itself was holding its breath.

The flames withered into thin, whispering tongues.

Corwin backed away, face pale, breath catching.

"It... it didn't like that."

Sir Aldric stood still, his eyes hollow. He didn't speak. He'd heard this kind of rage before: on the battlefield, in the dying gasps of men who knew they'd lost. But this was worse.

This was *cornered*.

And then a knock.

From outside the tower.

Thump.

Then again.

THUMP.

A third time, harder now, not a request but a demand.

The knights turned as one, toward the main door.

Then came the *voices*.

Muffled at first, like wind in a grave.

Then clearer.

"Let us in..."

"Please, I'm bleeding..."

"Why didn't you wait for me?"

"I fought beside you. *Open the door!*"

Corwin staggered. "That's... that's Joric. He died beside me. His throat..."

"I buried him," Thomelin said coldly. "These aren't the dead. They're *invitations*."

Aldric didn't move. His grip on his sword tightened, but he said nothing.

He had heard these voices already. And he knew now, they weren't going to stop.

THUMP. THUMP.

Then a *new voice*.

Calm. Cold. *Mocking*.

"Still breathing, are you?"

The words slithered through the cracks in the door like oil through stone.

It was the *stranger*. The man they'd let in.

Gone without a sound.

Now speaking from *outside*.

"Still pretending this tower can save you?" he whispered. "Still hoping for dawn?"

Thunder cracked overhead. The wind shrieked like laughter.

"You'll all die before sunrise."

A pause, thick with something too vast for breath.

"I've seen how it ends."

Another pause.

A grin, somehow audible in the dark.

"And so has *he*."

The wind cut off.

The voices stopped.

Silence took its place: deep and waiting.

And in that silence, the tower felt smaller. The fire colder. The night heavier.

The demon didn't have to break the door.

It was already inside their minds.

The last words from the stranger's voice ("And so has he") faded into the storm.

Then... silence.

The wind ceased.

The banging stopped.

The voices of the dead fell away like breath held too long.

Even the fire settled: low, quiet, no longer thrashing in fear.

The knights stood unmoving, waiting for the next strike of horror, but none came.

No one dared to break the silence in case it shattered.

Time passed: minutes, maybe ten. In that stillness, the horror almost felt like a fever breaking.

Had they endured it?

Had they *won*?

No one spoke.

The quiet felt earned. Like they'd passed through some kind of trial.

No screaming. No scratching. No tricks.

Just the crackling of flame, the whisper of tired rain, and the strange weightlessness of relief.

The torment had stopped, for now. No more whispers, no scratching at the door, no voices of the dead, no flickers of twisted visions in the fire. Only the low crackle of the flames and the steady roar of the storm pressing against the tower walls filled the silence. The knights sat slumped in the flickering light, armor smeared with blood and rain, eyes sunken from fear and fatigue. The stillness felt false, like a trap that hadn't sprung yet.

Sir Aldric, the eldest, shifted where he sat and broke the silence with a voice scraped raw by age and grief. "We should try and rest... before our friend starts again."

Corwin, the youngest, lifted his head slowly. "What about Sir Garran? Shouldn't we try to get him out?" His voice cracked. "He hasn't moved. I think he's..." He didn't finish.

Aldric didn't look up. He stared into the fire, eyes hollow. "He's gone. And it wants us in that room." His hand tightened around the hilt of his sword. "No. We rest. While we still can. It's going to be a long night."

6

Smoke, Splinters, and Strategy

Sir Aldric sat motionless, his back to the fire, eyes fixed on the shadows dancing along the cracked stone wall. The others thought him asleep, or at least lost in that dull, silent trance of grief he often wore like armor. But his eyes were open.

And somewhere deep behind them... he was far away.

Long ago, beneath another sun, the sky over Jerusalem had burned with smoke.

The clang of steel on steel had been endless then.

The air thick with smoke and screams, sunlight burned to gold behind rising ash. Stones shattered underfoot. Palms splintered. Crusaders roared through broken gates, and all around them the holy city wept.

Aldric had been young then. His sword arm still strong. His faith: shining, uncracked.

He remembered the weight of the chainmail biting into his shoulders, sweat stinging his eyes. His sword had been slick with blood, not the first time, not the last, but this fight had stayed with him.

The Saracen warrior had been quick. Young, but skilled. A curved blade in his hand, eyes sharp with fury and defiance. They had fought through the garden of a shattered temple: stones overturned, vines scorched black by fire. The world had shrunk to two men, each drawing breath between blows, each swing fueled by belief and rage.

Aldric had taken a cut to the thigh. It burned, but he pushed through it.

He remembered the final moment well.

The Saracen slipped, his foot catching on a broken urn, his balance gone for half a heartbeat. Aldric lunged, slammed the man to the ground, his sword pressed to the base of his throat.

The Saracen dropped his weapon and raised a shaking hand.

"*La... arjuq... la taqtulni...*" he pleaded. "Please... have mercy."

For a breath, Aldric hesitated.

The world narrowed to that moment. To the whispering wind through scorched olive trees. To the blood dripping from his own blade onto a stranger's chest.

Aldric could have spared him. Could have walked away. Could have turned his blade to the next threat.

Aldric stood over the Saracen, the man's outstretched hand trembling with desperation. For an instant, he felt the old ache of pity, suddenly the memory of Rennic rose behind his eyes, vivid as fresh blood: his son's body trampled in the dirt by Saracen horsemen, his pleas for mercy answered with iron. No quarter had been shown to the boy he had loved beyond all things. No softness. No reprieve. The pity in Aldric's chest curdled into rage. *They did not spare my only son,* he thought, jaw tightening, *why should I spare this man now?* His hand closed around the hilt.

He could have spared the Saracen.

Instead, he drove the sword down, slowly, deliberately, until the man stopped moving.

The man's breath left him with a soft sound, almost relief. Then he lay still, eyes open to the sky that had already turned its back.

He did not look away.

Aldric didn't speak. He stood. Wiped his blade. Walked on.

He told himself it was justice.

He told himself it was holy.

The blood had soaked into the temple floor, mingling with crushed petals and ash. For a moment, Aldric remembered thinking how quiet it was.

He had told himself it was war.

But something inside him had changed that day.

He had stopped hearing prayers clearly after that.

Back in the tower, the fire popped. The cold crept in again. Aldric blinked once, slow and tired, the memory slipping away like smoke. He stared at the flames, and for a moment, thought he saw the Saracen's face flicker within them: eyes wide, mouth half-open.

He rubbed at his jaw and muttered to no one:

"I could have spared him..."

But he hadn't.

And now, here in the dark, it felt like something had remembered.

Corwin sat close to the fire, legs drawn up, his arms wrapped around them like a child hiding from thunder. The rain beat steadily against the tower's crumbling stone, a cold rhythm that dulled the edges of his thoughts. For the first time in hours, the demon was silent.

No laughter.

No voices in the walls.

Only the wind howling through cracks like a breath held too long.

He stared at the fire, the flames dancing low. They cast soft light across the battered room, catching the iron band of the storage room door just enough to make it gleam. His eyes lingered there, on that door. On the thought of it bursting open, not with wind or rain, but something worse. Something *coming through*.

His heart beat faster.

So he looked away. Into the fire.

And slowly, the flames shifted.

The wind was warmer there. Softer. It smelled of hay and ripe apples.

He was home again, back in the cottage with the low beams and whitewashed walls. She stood at the window, pale hands pressed to the sill, staring out into the quiet fields.

Adelyne.

She turned as he entered, her eyes rimmed red but proud still. She was always proud. Even when she cried.

"You won't go, will you?" she asked, her voice barely above a whisper.

Corwin shook his head. "No," he said. "No, I won't go. Not to fight. I've no taste for war, nor call to it."

She smiled, just faintly. Relief tugged at her shoulders, and she stepped forward, resting her head against his chest.

"I don't care what others say," she whispered. "Let them speak of glory and crusade. I only care that you come back to me."

He held her there, breathing in the scent of her hair. Lavender and woodsmoke.

Then a floorboard creaked.

He looked up.

Her father stood in the doorway, arms crossed over his chest, the lines of an old soldier carved deep into his face. He said nothing until Adelyne had stepped away and gone to tend the hearth.

Then, quiet but sharp, he spoke.

"You'd turn your back on God's war?"

Corwin said nothing.

The older man stepped closer. "And if the heathens come here? If they burn our land, take our churches, defile the cross? Will you cower in the hayloft, boy?"

Corwin clenched his jaw.

"You love my daughter?" the man asked, voice now low. "Then be the man who can protect her. Not the coward who hides behind her skirts."

He turned to leave, but paused at the door, casting one last glance over his shoulder.

"If you won't fight for what's right," he said, voice like iron, "then you don't have my blessing. I won't see her marry a man afraid of his own shadow."

The words struck deeper than steel.

Later that night, Corwin stood by the stable, a packed satchel slung over his shoulder. His sword, new, still sharp, felt too heavy for its scabbard.

"You said you wouldn't go."

"I have to," Corwin said, forcing the words past the knot in his throat. "It's not just for glory. It's... it's for God. For us. I need to prove..."

She stepped back.

"You don't need to prove anything to me."

Adelyne stood by the gate, tears bright on her cheeks, her shawl clutched tight around her shoulders. The moon caught in her hair, silvering it like frost. To Corwin, she looked like something pulled from a prayer: too good for the world he was about to walk into.

He stepped closer, swallowing hard.

"You look like the last warm thing in the world," he whispered. "If heaven has a light, it looks like you."

She shook her head, fresh tears falling.

"Don't say things like that. Not when you're leaving."

He reached out and took her hand, pressing it to his chest.

"I'm going, Adelyne... but only to come back. I swear it. I'll return to you, with honor. With stories. With something worthy of the life we want to build. I'll wear your name like armor, and nothing will break it."

She tried to smile, but it broke halfway through.

"You don't need honor," she said. "You just need to live."

Then, without a word, she reached into the folds of her shawl and pulled something small and white from beneath it. A square of soft cloth, torn with care from the hem of the dress he'd gifted her last spring: the white one she'd worn on the day they first spoke of marriage beneath the apple trees.

She pressed it into his hand, folding his fingers over it.

"To remember," she said softly. "And to remind you where to return."

He looked down at it, then at her, eyes full of things too large to say.

He kissed her knuckles gently, then stepped away.

She didn't follow.

He looked back only once, and saw her still standing there: small, still, heartbreak in her eyes as he rode into the pale light of dawn.

Now, in the tower, the fire hissed and twisted. Corwin blinked, the memory fading like smoke through fingers. He felt the scrap of white cloth pressed to his chest: hers. The last thing she gave him.

Rain poured harder now. The storage room door creaked under the weight of wind.

He wondered, not for the first time, if he had come to war for her...

...or just to silence the voice that called him coward.

Sir Garran stirred.

A breath caught in his throat: wet, rattling. Pain lanced up through his ribs, his spine, his left leg. Every nerve screamed as he tried to move.

The world around him was black... almost.

A thin tongue of firelight leaked through the narrow hole in the storage room door, casting a faint, flickering line across the floor. Dust hung in the air like ash. Somewhere behind him, the stones were damp with blood: his.

He tried to move again.

His leg wouldn't respond.

Broken, he thought dimly. Or worse.

The last thing he remembered was the heat of rage: charging into the dark, sword raised, voice raw from shouting.

The thing had been waiting.

It hadn't struck him like a beast. It hadn't lunged.

It had *watched* him come.

And then the pain.

Bones shattered. Armor torn like parchment. Flesh split like fruit under steel.

But why wasn't he dead?

Why am I still breathing?

He lay half on his side, staring at the faint glow on the floor. He couldn't see the creature. Couldn't hear it.

But it was here. Somewhere in the dark.

And the thought slid into his mind like a knife:

Am I bait?

Did it leave me alive so the others would come?

Do they think I'm already dead?

His fingers twitched. Grit scraped beneath his nails as he dug them into the floor and began to *crawl*.

Every inch was agony. His breath came in short, broken gasps. Blood dripped from his mouth.

He turned slowly onto his front, teeth clenched against the pain, and pulled himself forward, away from the darkest part of the chamber. The cage stood there, just beyond where the firelight reached. Its corner gleamed faintly, catching the orange edge of torchlight.

Was it still inside?

Was it watching him?

Something moved.

A soft sound, like skin sliding over stone. Or something *else*.

He stopped. Waited.

Nothing.

He kept crawling. Reaching. Pulling.

After a lifetime of pain, he reached the far wall and slumped against it. His back hit cold stone. He slid down it, half-collapsed, breathing ragged and shallow.

He couldn't call out. His voice was gone. His chest ached with every breath, and his leg... he couldn't feel it anymore.

The flicker of firelight still touched the edge of the cage.

His eyes didn't leave it.

If he was going to die... he wanted to see it coming.

And as the dark held him in its teeth, his thoughts slid *backward*, to a time when pain had been simpler. Bruises. Pride. Lessons learned with fists instead of claws.

He had been a boy again.

The summer sun glared over a dusty field, wooden swords in hand. His older brother, *Merren*, was taller, stronger. They circled each other while their father, grizzled, silent, watched from a stump with arms crossed.

The clash came quick. Garran swung wild. Merren caught the blow.

Garran hit the dirt hard, nose bloodied, eyes watering, but he was still awake.

Still breathing.

Before he could rise, his father stood.

"To win," the old man said sharply, "*you finish it.*"

Merren looked down at his brother, uncertain. Breathing hard.

"Finish it," the old man growled. "*No mercy. You'll get none in this world.*"

Merren's face twisted with anger: at their father, at the lesson, at the world. And he struck.

A punch to Garran's jaw.

Another to the cheek.

Then fists, heavy, hot with fury, hammering until Garran stopped moving.

He woke hours later, blood crusted over his brow, flies buzzing near his lip. The sun was low now. The air smelled like sweat and dirt.

His father stood above him.

"You gave up too easy," he said coldly.

Then he walked away, leaving his son in the dust, staring up at the sky.

Years passed.

Another fight, this one inside a grimy tavern, stinking of ale and sweat. Garran was no longer a boy.

The man across from him was big. Drunk. Mean.

The fight had started with words, spilled into fists. Chairs crashed.

Garran's lip split. Blood filled his mouth. The man struck again. And again.

The drunk hit Garran with a chair. He fell to the ground.

He *rose*.

Again.

And again.

Each blow rattled his bones. But nothing broke the fire in his eyes.

He would not give up.

Not anymore.

They could beat him bloody, leave him crawling, spit in his face, but they'd have to *kill* him to make him stop.

Back in the tower, Garran stared into the dark, ribs aching, leg numb, chest rising in shallow gasps.

The cage was still there.

And maybe so was the thing.

But he was *still breathing*.

And until that stopped,

He wasn't done.

Not yet.

Sir Thomelin sat with his arms folded, one hand absently resting on the hilt of his sheathed sword, the other draped across his knee. His eyes were locked on the storage room door.

The storm outside had not let up, but within the tower, the silence had returned: tense, uncertain. The others shifted restlessly, haunted by visions and voices, but Thomelin sat still, mind grinding like a millstone behind steady eyes.

It had been hours. Or perhaps minutes. The flow of time had fractured.

He studied the door. The iron bolts. The floor around it. The warping of the torchlight in its seams. The faint smell of damp earth and something worse: like rot left too long in a sealed cellar.

The night made no sense.

So he searched for shape. For logic. For *patterns.*

And the firelight flickered.

And his mind, ever reaching, ever dissecting, slipped into memory.

It had been summer.

The field stretched wide beneath a cloudless sky, the scent of clover and sun-warmed grass thick in the breeze. A wooden table sat beneath a tree, and on it, a chessboard. Simple carved pieces, smoothed by years of use.

He sat across from Master Edric: his mentor, his teacher in both letters and swordwork. The man's beard was white, but his eyes still gleamed with sharpness and humor.

"You think too much," Edric would often say, "but sometimes, that's a blessing."

They were deep into the match. Thomelin, younger, eager, had just moved his knight into a bold, forward position, grinning as he did.

"There," he said. "Pressure on your bishop, and a clear path to your king."

Edric raised a single eyebrow.

"Oh?" he said mildly.

Then, with the gentlest flick of his fingers, he slid his queen across the board.

"Checkmate."

Thomelin blinked. Looked down. Then back up, stunned.

"But..."

"You focused on the attack," Edric said, smiling. "You were so pleased with your pressure, you forgot to protect your own lines."

Edric chuckled and tapped the board.

"What's the lesson?"

Thomelin frowned, thinking. Then: "That a bold strike means nothing if it leaves you open?"

"Aye," Edric nodded. "But deeper than that. Patience, Thomelin. Patience sees the whole board. Reckless men draw blades first. But wise men wait... and watch. The game belongs to the one who lets his enemy move first, and *then* makes the only move that matters."

They both laughed. A breeze stirred the leaves overhead. It was a perfect day.

And then a sound like the earth itself being torn apart.

A *roar*: deep, blood-soaked, unnatural, ripped through the tower, tearing Thomelin out of the memory like a blade through cloth.

The storage room door *shuddered,* the iron bolts groaning. From within, something snarled: a wet, choking growl, not quite animal and not quite man.

The others rose in alarm. Steel hissed from scabbards.

Thomelin was already standing.

His breath came slow.

He looked once more at the sealed door and whispered to himself:

"Let it rage. We will move last."

7

Bargain in the Dark

Darkness pressed against his skin like wet cloth. The air was thick with rot and cold stone, his breath shallow and ragged as he slumped against the far wall. Pain still roared through his leg: a dull, pulsing throb that never quite faded. Somewhere above, the tower groaned in the wind, bones shifting in the storm.

He didn't know how long he'd been unconscious. Minutes. Hours. Maybe longer.

Then:

A voice.

Not loud.

Not close.

But *in* the room.

In *him*.

"Garran..."

The name floated through the dark like a drop of blood in water.

Drawn out. Syllables curled in velvet and smoke.

"Garrrran..."

He stiffened, back pressing harder to the cold stone behind him. The pain in his leg flared like coals, but he did not cry out. He clenched his teeth and stared into the dark where the cage stood: a blacker shape in blackness, just barely visible where the dying torchlight spilled through the hole in the door beyond.

The voice came again. Gentle. Amused.

"Look in the cage."

Garran didn't move.

"What game are you playing, demon?" His voice was hoarse, thick with pain, but steady.

The reply came faster. Harder. A crack of malice beneath the calm.

"*Look... in the cage.*"

He said nothing.

The silence deepened.

Then, sharper now. Hungrier.

"*Look in the cage or I'll kill you all.* One by one. The boy first. Then the clever one. Then your priest of war. I'll rip their souls out through their teeth. *Look in the cage.*"

Garran's fists clenched.

He didn't believe it. He *couldn't* believe it.

But something in the voice...

Something knew it was already in his blood.

He turned his head, eyes squinting through the dark. The cage stood across the chamber, just beyond the reach of the flame. A bent, jagged shadow, veiled in deeper black.

The floor was slick beneath his hands as he dragged himself toward it, inch by inch. His wounded leg screamed with every movement. The cold was sharper here. The air felt *wet*, like something breathing against his neck.

As he moved closer, he heard it.

Breathing.

Low. Heavy. Animal.

A sound like lungs too big for their cage, dragging in air through something wet and wrong.

He froze.

Then crawled on.

The cage loomed now, just a few feet away.

The torchlight from the hall flickered weakly through the hole, sending orange ripples over the iron bars.

He swallowed.

Forced himself upright (knees wobbling, pain dancing behind his eyes) and leaned forward.

"Now what, demon?" he rasped. "I've looked."

No answer.

The breathing had stopped.

He leaned closer.

The bars were cold. Wet with condensation. Something else.

He peered into the dark beyond them.

Nothing moved.

His eyes narrowed.

No shape.

No form.

Just...

His breath caught.

The cage... was *empty*.

Garran blinked, pulled back slightly.

No.

No, that couldn't be right.

He pushed forward again, heart racing now.

The canvas they had thrown over it was gone. The iron bar on the far side lay where it had been placed. The straw was flattened. Streaked with blood. But the space within the bars was hollow.

Void. *Empty.*

"The cage is empty..." he breathed. Then louder, anger clawing back into his voice. "Where are you hiding, demon?! Come into the light and I'll grant you a swift death."

The reply came not from the cage, but from all around him.

A laugh.

Low. Cruel. Like a child mocking a prayer.

Then, the voice returned: silken, serpentine.

"The light won't protect you."

The words slithered into his ear like a cold wind through bone.

"I'll make you a deal, knight..."

The tone changed: syrupy and slow, like an offer wrapped in poison.

"Pick one of your friends in the other room."

A pause.

"Pick one... to die."

Garran's breath caught.

"You will be spared," the demon purred. "I will let you go. Your wound healed. Your sins forgiven. You may walk free, knight. Just choose."

A silence stretched, taut as a drawn bowstring.

"Pick one, Garran," it whispered again.

"Pick one."

Pick one, Garran.

Silence stretched, until Garran shifted, bracing himself on the cage's iron frame, and forced a sharp breath between his teeth.

"I'm not playing your games," he growled. "If you want blood, take mine."

He dragged himself upright against the bars, trembling but unbowed.

"Unless you fear me."

A pause.

Then *laughter*.

Low and thick, like rot bubbling through a well.

"Fear you?" the demon hissed, amused. "No, knight. I know you. Brave, battered Garran. Always the fist, never the mind."

The voice curved, curling into his ear with sickly warmth.

"But don't you want to go home?" it whispered. "All it will cost you is one name. Just *one*. Say it, and this ends. No more pain. No more dark."

The air grew colder.

"You don't even *like* them, do you? You barely know them. You bled beside them, but for what? Glory? Gold? A bishop's empty promise?"

A pause.

"They won't know. They'll never know you picked. You can still live."

Then, soft as breath through bone:

"Say a name."

Garran didn't flinch.

He pushed off the bars, standing crooked but tall, blood dripping from his chin. His voice came low, steady, iron-willed.

"Then I pick me."

The air tightened.

"You can't tempt me, demon. My faith in God is resolute. His will, not yours, shall be done."

He took one step forward into the dark.

"If I lose... if I die here..."

A faint smile touched his broken lips.

"...then I'm guaranteed my place in heaven." Garran holds his cross up in defiance.

Silence followed.

Then, from the shadows behind the cage, came a sound like grinding teeth over stone, and something new beneath the laugh:

"Still clutching your cross like it means something. Still thinking that suffering refines the soul, that obedience earns paradise. How small your world must be, boxed in by sermons and fear."

The voice seemed to get angrier and closer from the darkness.

"Have you never wondered why your prayers echo back empty? Why heaven stays silent even as you bleed in its name? The truth, little knight, is not that your god is absent... but that he was never worthy."

"You kneel to him. You kill for him. And in return, he gives you war, rot, and silence. But I... I offer something better. Knowledge. The kind that burns through the veil and shows you the machinery behind your little heaven. The kind that frees you from the wheel of guilt and slaughter. Taste it, and you'll see the truth: your salvation was never real. Only the leash around your neck was."

"I'm fighting for God's will, this is a *holy war* against infidels. When I die demon I will be absolved of all sins, my ticket guaranteed to heaven," Garran tries to convince himself.

"Faith is for beasts. But you, knight... you could be more than that. If only you'd dare to look."

"I'd die first and I'll take as much of you with me when I go."

Garran shifted, breath ragged, jaw clenched tight against the pain that gnawed at his leg like fire on bone. Blood had dried tacky down one side of his face, and every movement lit his ribs with fresh agony.

The dark pressed close, thick as pitch, broken only by the dull ember-glow leaking from the hole in the storage room door.

Then, again, the voice.

Low. Patient. Closer now.

"Garran... You're bleeding out. Can't move. Can't fight. Your friends have left you to die in the dark."

Garran bared his teeth. "Still breathing, aren't I?"

The voice laughed: soft, wet. Not mocking... indulgent.

"Barely. And for what? Glory? Loyalty? Some brittle faith that cracks the moment you scream?"

"You know why I left you breathing?" the demon whispered.

He didn't answer.

"Because I wanted you to hear this."

Another pause.

"Pick one. Just one. Name a knight. Any of them. Say the name, and I'll let you live."

Garran grit his teeth. "You won't break me."

"Won't I?"

The voice slithered, slick with something ancient and hollow.

"You hate Aldric. His tired old eyes judging you. You hate Thomelin, always thinking, always watching, like he's better than you. And Corwin..."

A dark chuckle.

"So young. So soft. He'll die screaming. Say his name. End this."

He lifted the small iron cross that hung from his neck, bent now, stained with blood.

"I pick me," he said through bloodied lips. "Take me. I won't trade their lives. I won't kneel to a thing like you."

Silence.

Then the voice coiled close, just behind his ear.

"Then kneel to your silence. Your prayers will rot in your mouth."

But Garran smiled, just slightly.

"I'll die on my feet."

8

The Faith That Binds

The fire had burned low. Its once-golden glow had dulled to red coals and dancing shadows, the kind that crept up walls and clung to the edges of armor like soot-stained ghosts. Rain battered the tower's stones. Thunder rolled like the growl of something older than the sky.

Sir Aldric sat nearest the hearth, cross resting against his knee, his eyes fixed on the door to the storage room.

Then, soft as ash falling on a grave, came a sound.

A presence.

Something moved in the shadows behind the fire.

A shape. A figure.

Aldric blinked. The fire was flickering wrong: too steady, too slow. As if time inside the flames had changed its mind.

For a moment, he let his eyes slip closed, wishing he could sink fully into the dark. But then came the voice.

Soft at first. Like a memory spoken aloud.

"Aldric..."

His name drifted across the room in that velvet rasp that made the skin behind his ears prickle. He didn't answer. He only clenched the iron cross in his fist until the edges bit blood.

"You are tired," the demon murmured. The voice oozed from the sealed storage room, thick as smoke. "You pretend you sit here in faith, but I know the ache in your marrow. You came here for vengeance, old knight, not for God."

Aldric's jaw tensed. He stared into the fire. "Your words are shadows. They cannot sway me."

"No?" the thing crooned. The walls seemed to lean closer to listen. "Then why does your heart beat faster when I speak his name?"

Silence stretched.

"You pray to silence," Caelomin went on, a note of pity slithering through the mockery. "You kneel to a throne that never held a king. Your god is not absent. He is irrelevant. He is the husk left when men needed a father to absolve them."

The flames guttered low, licking the edges of the hearth as if they, too, feared the voice.

"You say you fight for Him," Caelomin continued, each word slow as dripping wax. "But you are here because your son rots beneath a cairn of stones in a land he never knew."

Aldric's breath caught. His hand twitched over the cross, squeezing it hard enough to whiten the knuckles.

"The silence you worship," Caelomin whispered, "never protected your boy."

"Stop," Aldric rasped.

"I could have protected him."

Aldric's gaze lifted at last, meeting the iron-banded door with eyes hollowed by too many winters. "You lie," he said hoarsely. "You twist all things to your foul purpose."

"But the truth is so simple," the demon sighed, its voice curling around the rafters like smoke. "He died screaming for a god who never answered. Do you want to know why?"

Aldric did not speak.

"Because that god," Caelomin said, voice now cold and grand as a cathedral's vault, "abandoned men and their sons long before your precious crusade ever set sail. The holy light you cling to is spent. All that remains is the dark between stars."

The wind screamed outside, rattling the tower's bones. Aldric pressed a hand to his chest as though to keep something from clawing out.

"Why?" he whispered finally. "If He is just, if He is merciful, why did my boy die alone on a forgotten field in His name?"

Silence. A silence so complete it felt like the world itself was holding its breath.

Then the voice returned, softer than ever:

"Because He does not care."

Aldric's throat worked.

"He did not hear your son's cries," Caelomin went on, each syllable laid with dreadful care. "He does not hear yours. I could show you, if you wished. The moment your boy passed into the dark."

"No."

The word was ragged. Weak.

"I could show you," Caelomin persisted, "how he really died. Not in valor. Not in piety. But in fear."

Aldric shook his head, but his vision had begun to blur.

"Shall I show you?" the demon purred.

And before he could answer, the fire died.

In the blackness behind his eyes, the vision bloomed.

He saw his son, Rennic, standing in a smoky tavern, not on a battlefield. A clay cup in one hand, unshaven, eyes glassy with drink. Another knight stumbled into him: broad-shouldered, bearded, reeking of sour ale. Garran. They argued (words lost to the phantom wind) and then Garran shoved him. Hard.

Rennic fell. Struck his head on a stone bench. His eyes widened, then went dull.

"No..." Aldric whispered. "No, he fell at Arsuf. He..."

"Watch," Caelomin urged.

The scene rippled. Garran knelt by Rennic's side, voice cracking, hands trembling. Blood pooled beneath the boy's hair, slow as spilled wine. Garran's lips shaped apologies: too late, too weak.

The vision twisted again. Now Garran stood over the body, a half-empty cup dangling from his fist. The tavern's candles guttered out, and darkness swallowed all but Rennic's open, empty eyes.

The light returned with a gasp that scraped Aldric's lungs raw. The fire was back. The tower as it was. But his hands shook.

He stared at Garran, who lay slumped by the far wall, unaware.

"You see?" Caelomin breathed. "Your son didn't die in holy battle. He died in filth, in drink, in ignorance."

Aldric closed his eyes. He was weeping. "No. You show lies."

"They are truths your faith cannot stomach. Let me show you more," Caelomin coaxed. "Let me peel back the last illusions. You need only to ask."

In the corner of the tower where the shadows gathered thickest, *someone stood.*

The figure stood near the wall. Slender. Young. The face half-shadowed but achingly familiar.

"Rennic..."

His voice cracked like old timber.

The boy didn't speak. Just watched.

There was dirt on his face. His armor was dented in the same place Aldric remembered: the left pauldron, crushed by a warhammer in a siege long past.

"You're not real," Aldric said quietly. "I buried you. Myself."

Aldric rose slowly. The others didn't notice. They didn't *see*.

He stepped closer, heart thundering.

The boy tilted his head.

His lips parted, not in speech, but to reveal the black movement of *insects* beneath the skin. Maggots, writhing in his mouth, falling softly to the floor.

Aldric reeled back, breath choking in his throat.

He blinked, and the figure was gone.

But he could still hear them. The soft *wet* sound of maggots chewing.

Somewhere. Beneath the floor.

Corwin pressed the white cloth to his chest like a relic.

Corwin heard it next.

A voice: soft, clean, warm.

"Corwin..."

His head snapped up.

He knew that voice.

He rose and walked to the narrow arrow slit in the wall, heart pounding. He looked out.

And there, just beyond the firelight, she stood.

Wearing her dress. White. Flowing.

Rain touched nothing. Wind ignored her.

She held a torch: its flame not flickering *outward*, but *inward*, drawn into the wood as though devoured by its own fire.

"Come home," she whispered, hand reaching toward him.

Corwin's heart shattered. He pressed against the stone.

Then her skin began to *unravel.*

Thread by thread. Her face came apart, like fabric rotting in real time, until only hollow eyes stared back.

He screamed and fell away from the wall.

But when he looked again, there was only the rain.

And the dark.

And the empty fields.

Thomelin had been staring at the fire, trying to measure his breathing.

Thomelin turned as he heard something behind him.

A voice. Not the demon's.

A voice.

"Blessed are the broken..."

It came from nowhere and everywhere: deep, familiar.

He turned and saw the *shadow* first, a pulpit's silhouette stretched across the far wall.

But there was no pulpit.

No speaker.

Still, the sermon continued.

"They shall suffer, and in their suffering, be consumed."

It was the bishop's cadence, but the words were twisted.

"To burn is to serve. To be devoured is to be known."

Thomelin drew his blade, turning toward the wall, but the shadow pulpit remained unmoving.

He stepped forward.

The fire hissed behind him.

The voice grew quiet, but clearer.

"You're already kneeling, Thomelin. You just haven't looked down yet... kneel before Caelomin!"

He stopped.

And glanced at his feet.

His knees were bent, slightly.

Unknowingly.

As if he *had* knelt.

The air around Thomelin thickened like smoke with weight. The sermon rolled on, each word a needle threading through his spine.

"To doubt is to see. And to see is to suffer."

The bishop's voice... no, not quite. It *wore* his voice like a mask. It spoke with too many mouths: some behind him, some beneath.

Thomelin tried to rise.

His legs didn't move.

He looked down.

His knees weren't bent.

They were *rooted*.

Stone, moss-black and cold, had crept up from the cracks in the floor, coiling around his legs like old vines. Holding him. Feeding on him. His fingers reached for his blade, but his hands were no longer gripping it.

They were folded.

In prayer.

The fire dimmed. Not died: dimmed, as if shamed.

And from the shadow of the pulpit came a new shape. A figure cloaked in clerical robes, but too tall, too thin, too still. The hood hung low over where a face should be, and from beneath it, pale fingers dripped something dark and sticky onto the floor: blood, or ink, or both.

"You sought wisdom," the figure said, voice dry as dust. *"You sought truth through reason. But truth was never yours to wield."*

The walls of the tower stretched, the firelight pulling away as if repelled. The stones wept old blood. The bishop's voice (or the thing that wore it) spoke again:

"Do not rise, child. The weight you feel is faith."

The bishop's voice, dry and cracked, echoed like a whisper through a crypt.

The robed figure stepped forward.

Its feet didn't touch the floor.

And from within its robes, it drew something long and curved, gleaming darkly in the firelight.

A dagger.

Old. Bronze or bone. Etched with runes that writhed if looked at too long.

The blade dripped.

Already wet.

Blood slid down it slow as oil, as if time bled too.

Thomelin's breath caught. He tried again to move, but the stone coiled tighter around his knees. His hands remained folded, no longer by choice. The fire hissed behind him, casting his shadow long against the far wall. The other knights seemingly can't see what is happening.

"You built your house on logic, child," it whispered, bringing the dagger up (ever so slowly) to rest against the side of Thomelin's neck.

"You thought understanding would shield you. That reason was light enough to banish what waits in the dark."

The blade was cold.

Too cold.

"You trusted in your mind. Your sacred texts. Your bishop's words. But here you kneel... alone... unarmed... unloved."

"Tell me, Thomelin..." the voice breathed into his ear.

"...where is your God now?"

The dagger pressed tighter, not cutting, not yet, but close enough that his pulse thudded against the edge.

"He does not speak. He does not save. He sends you to die beneath broken towers, chasing devils he cannot cage."

"You called yourself a thinker. A man of structure, of truth. But you came to war for faith, not reason. And now both abandon you."

A beat of silence. Rain lashed the tower.

"There is no logic here. Only submission."

"Bow, Thomelin. Not in duty. Not in pride. In truth. In surrender."

"Give me your mind. And I will free you from the burden of having one."

Thomelin did not flinch.

The blade trembled at his throat, but he lifted his eyes slowly into the face of the bishop. The firelight reflected nothing in its hood but shadow, deeper than night.

His voice came out low, hoarse, but firm:

"You're not real."

A silence.

The bishop's head tilted, curious.

"You're an illusion... An illusion conjured by something too afraid to face us as it truly is."

The dagger pressed harder. A thin trickle of blood welled, warm against his skin.

Still, he went on.

"If you were real, if your creature was as powerful as it claims, we'd already be dead. It would have torn us apart, fed on our marrow, danced in our blood."

His breath hitched, but he steadied it.

"But we are still here."

A pause. The bishop did not speak.

Thomelin's voice grew stronger, louder, cutting through the dark like a bell rung for the dying.

"You speak of submission. Of inevitability. Of silence. But even your logic betrays you."

"Because if you exist, if devils walk this earth, then so does your opposite."

He raised his chin, just slightly. The blade caught the motion, scraped a hair's breadth of skin, but he didn't stop. He felt himself becoming more free from the ground.

"If there is evil... then there is good. If there is hell, then heaven awaits."

The wind screamed against the tower. The fire roared. Still he spoke:

"You can kill me. Tear me limb from limb. But I'll see my brothers again. I'll hold my mother's hand in the light. I'll walk with the saints beneath skies you'll never know."

His lip curled, not in fear, but in scorn.

"You will be alone. In the cold and darkness. Forever."

The bishop's shadow did not move.

Thomelin leaned forward, into the blade now.

"So go ahead. Cut me. But know this: each drop of blood you spill brings me closer to the only truth you cannot touch."

The flames behind him surged high. The dagger shook.

And for the first time, the bishop stepped back.

Then, without sound or motion, the figure vanished.

No gust of wind. No flash of flame.

Just... gone.

As if it had never been there at all.

The oppressive weight that had pinned Thomelin to the stones suddenly lifted. The cold shackles that bound his knees to the floor cracked like dry ice and broke apart in silence, melting into dust that faded before it hit the ground.

He gasped, his breath returning all at once, ragged and sharp. The blood on his neck felt warm again, real. The air rushed back into his lungs.

The tower around him came into focus.

He straightened with a gasp and turned, but the shadow was gone.

The fire popped behind him.

Nothing but stone.

And silence.

The three knights remained, each quiet, each haunted.

None spoke of what they saw.

And though the darkness still pressed in from the corners, it no longer felt invincible.

He wiped the blood from his throat with shaking fingers and stood slowly, his legs weak but holding.

Somewhere behind the door, the demon still watched.

But for now... it had blinked first.

9
When the March Began

Sir Thomelin stood slowly, his breath still ragged, the blood from his neck already drying in a thin line across his skin. His voice, when it came, was low, but certain.

"I saw it," he said. "Not with my eyes... but I saw it. It took the form of someone I trusted. Twisted his words. Tried to break me."

The others turned. Corwin looked up from where he'd been clutching the white scrap of cloth. Aldric's gaze didn't leave the fire, but his hand tightened around the cross resting on his knee.

"You too?" Corwin whispered. "I... I saw Adelyne. Outside the tower. She spoke to me. Her face..." He stopped, swallowing hard. "And then it unraveled. Like she was made of thread and rot."

Aldric didn't speak for a long moment.

Then, without turning, he muttered, "Rennic. My boy. His armor still dented where the hammer crushed it. Maggots in his mouth." His eyes flicked to the flames. "I buried him myself."

The fire crackled low.

Outside, the storm groaned against the walls, and within the tower, nothing moved. No whispers now. No laughter.

Just the hiss of rainfall on stone, and the dim, flickering firelight painting long, uncertain shadows.

"It's too quiet," Thomelin muttered.

Corwin nodded. "We should leave. Now. Before it tries again."

"No," Aldric said at once, his voice harder now. "We run, we lose shelter. There could be enemy patrols out there. And that storm's not letting up."

Corwin turned on him, eyes wide, voice trembling with barely-contained fear. "I'd rather take my chances in the rain, with Saracen blades at my throat, than sit in here another hour with that thing clawing through my mind!"

Thomelin stepped between them. "It's not as strong as you think," he said. "It hasn't harmed us, not directly. Everything it's done has been with words, with visions. Smoke and shadow. Mind games."

Then a growl.

Low.

Deep.

Wrong.

The knights froze.

Their heads turned together toward the storage room door.

It creaked.

Just a touch.

Not pushed.

Not opened.

Just the sound of strained wood, as if something inside shifted its weight.

Silence followed.

Then movement.

A shuffle.

A scrape.

The growl came again. Louder. Older. Hungrier.

The knights rose in unison. Blades hissed from sheaths, steel catching the firelight.

The storage room door exploded open, slamming back against the stone.

They stood ready: swords raised, breath held, eyes wide.

But nothing came out.

Only blackness.

The darkness within the room was heavier than it should have been: thick, like smoke clinging to flesh. The shadows didn't shift. They waited.

Then movement.

A figure emerged.

Staggering. Limping. A shape half-silhouetted in the firelight.

The knights tensed.

This was it.

Whatever it was, whatever horror waited behind that veil of shadow, it was coming.

They braced themselves. Prayed for a swift death. Prayed for their souls to hold.

Then the figure stumbled forward, one arm dragging, blood smeared across the chest.

"Garran!" Corwin shouted.

He collapsed to the floor with a grunt, breath rattling in his lungs.

The others surged forward, swords forgotten for now.

Aldric dropped to one knee beside him. "Garran, what happened? Speak, man!"

Garran's eyes fluttered open. He coughed, once (wet and thick) and whispered:

"...it tried to make me choose..."

His voice cracked. He passed out.

The Sound Came Like a Wound Opening.

A horn.

Faint at first (drawn thin by distance and storm) but unmistakable. A low, echoing note that coiled through the rain like something wounded calling home.

Sir Thomelin turned his head sharply, rising from where he'd been seated. His hand found the hilt of his blade by instinct, though he did not yet draw it. Aldric was already on his feet, moving with the slow caution of an old wolf who's seen too many snares.

They moved to the arrow slit, side by side, peering out through the rain-smeared stone.

Corwin did not move.

He sat still by the fire, the scrap of white cloth clutched in his hands, eyes unfocused, mouth slightly open. A trance held him: whether born of exhaustion, horror, or something worse, they did not know.

Behind them, Garran remained unconscious, his breathing shallow. Blood soaked the makeshift bandage on his leg.

Outside, the storm howled.

And in its curtain of grey, they saw them.

Figures.

Five... six... more?

Shadows against the deeper dark, stepping slowly out of the treeline, their shapes warped by distance and rain. Men. Armed. Some with helmets. Others bare-headed. All with the Bishop's sigil (a white flame on crimson) painted onto shields and torn cloaks.

Sir Aldric narrowed his eyes.

"They're early," he muttered. "Too early. Reinforcements weren't due till after sunrise."

Thomelin didn't answer. He was squinting harder now, trying to trace their shapes.

The figures had stopped just beyond the muddy slope that led to the tower. Maybe twenty paces from the base. They didn't call out. Didn't raise a banner. Didn't move.

They simply stood.

Staring.

Their faces half-obscured by shadow and storm, but even in this pale light, something was wrong. Their postures were crooked, leaning slightly to one side. Their arms hung too still. One of them held a spear that trembled, not with the wind, but with some inner rhythm, like his hand shook in time with a heartbeat not his own.

Aldric leaned forward slightly.

"Something's off."

Thomelin nodded. "Their stances... they're not right. Like they're waiting for orders they've already forgotten."

One of the figures shifted suddenly, too quickly. A jolt, like a puppet jerked by a frayed string.

Another tilted its head at an unnatural angle, as if listening for a sound no one else could hear.

"They haven't moved since we saw them," Thomelin muttered. "They're just standing there... watching."

"They're not calling out," Aldric said. "No greeting. No sign. Just... silence."

"Could be scouts," Thomelin offered, though his tone lacked conviction. "Sent ahead."

"Then where are the horses? Where's the rest of the column?" Aldric's eyes narrowed. "We didn't send word. No one should be here. Not yet."

Another long silence followed. The wind pressed harder against the tower walls. The rain fell colder.

Then the figures moved.

Not forward.

Not away.

They began to march in place.

Feet lifted and dropped in perfect rhythm. Not stepping toward the tower, but hammering the ground beneath them. A drumbeat made of meat and iron.

Thud. Thud. Thud.

Weapons were raised, not in salute, but in mimicry. A spear pounded the mud like a flagellant's lash. A sword clanged against a shield in jagged time. Another figure began to nod its head slowly with each beat, like it was keeping tempo for a song only it could hear.

Thud. Thud. Thud.

The sound echoed up the ridge, carried on rain and wind, distorted by distance into something that felt older than war.

Aldric took a step back from the window, his face ashen.

"They're not here to help us," he said.

Thomelin didn't answer.

He was still watching.

Still counting.

And the figures below... were still staring.

Still marching.

Still smiling.

And the storm had stopped screaming.

Only the sound of boots in mud remained.

Thud. Thud. Thud.

Then, all at once, they stopped.

Every one of them.

Motionless again.

As if awaiting a signal.

As if listening.

As if they knew they were being watched.

And then, together, they looked up.

Straight at the arrow slit.

Straight at the tower.

Straight at them.

Sir Thomelin whispered:

"...I don't think they're breathing."

Meanwhile...

Corwin hadn't moved.

He sat by the fire, his eyes fixed and glassy, the scrap of white cloth still crumpled tight in his fists. The horn had not stirred him. The frantic footfalls of the knights, the clatter of steel, the rush to the window: none of it reached him.

It was as though something had taken hold.

His breath came shallow. His posture was too still. Not the stillness of sleep, or even prayer: something stranger. Unnatural.

As if his soul were staring at something the others could not see.

Then he moved.

Slowly. Silently.

His limbs unfolded like a man underwater, and he rose to his feet with the aching weight of a dreamer who did not know he'd slept.

Around him, time had unraveled.

The crackling of the fire fell away.

The drumming of the rain on stone ceased.

Even the thunder seemed held behind glass.

Sir Aldric and Thomelin stood at the arrow slit, frozen: mid-turn, mid-breath, as if locked in wax. They did not speak. Did not blink. Did not even notice as Corwin turned from the fire and began to walk.

He didn't understand why he was moving.

Only that he must.

His eyes drifted toward the storage room and stopped.

The door was wide open.

10

The Unveiling

Where before there had been only shadow and horror, now a brilliant white light poured forth: radiant and pulsing, as if the sun itself had descended into the heart of the storm.

It wasn't harsh.

It was beautiful.

Warm.

Alive.

It flowed out of the doorway like breath, like song, like something sacred trying to push back the dark.

Corwin shielded his eyes, blinking fast against the overwhelming brightness.

"Aldric?" he called out, voice trembling. "Are you seeing this? The light, do you see it?"

No response.

The older knight didn't turn.

Neither did Thomelin.

They stood like statues in a world that had stopped turning.

Corwin's breath caught.

He took a step toward the open door.

The warmth kissed his face, soft and golden.

And within the light...

...a shape began to form.

A silhouette.

Graceful. Familiar.

And then he saw her.

Adelyne.

She stood just inside the threshold, bathed in white. Her dress (the same white gown from their last night beneath the trees) fluttered gently, untouched by wind. Her hair glowed like woven starlight. Her eyes shone with peace. She looked exactly as he remembered her. No, more than that.

She looked perfect.

"Corwin," she whispered, her voice like the first light of dawn. "You found me."

He staggered forward a half-step, overwhelmed. His knees nearly buckled.

She raised a hand (palm open) and beckoned him closer.

"Come to me. It's safe here. The pain will end. You've done enough."

Corwin's mouth trembled. He was crying. He hadn't realized.

He stepped closer.

But even in the beauty, even in the warmth, some scrap of his mind remained his.

He stopped just short of the threshold.

The warmth pressed against his skin like sunlight through stained glass, but something deep inside him (older than reason) held him still.

He stared into the light, trembling.

"Are you..." His voice caught. He swallowed. "Are you demon or delusion?"

She tilted her head, her smile unchanged, but her eyes no longer wept with love.

"It's not a demon," she said.

But her voice changed.

With each word, it twisted: richer, heavier, the sweetness draining like wine turning to rot. Her tone deepened, thickened, pulled itself through thorns.

"It was summoned here."

The light behind her dimmed.

"It was called..."

Her outline began to warp.

The white glow yellowed.

Then greyed.

Then bled.

Her skin, once soft and glowing, seemed stretched now: like wax over something moving beneath.

"Come closer," the voice rasped.

The brilliance faded almost completely now, leaving only a sickly halo flickering at the edges.

"I was a servant of Heaven," the voice said (deeper now, fractured, like stone cracking underwater).

Corwin stepped back in horror.

The thing that had worn her face now stood in its own shape: a tall, withered figure wrapped in white that had turned to ash, its features shifting behind layers of burned beauty.

The light behind it guttered, pulsing like a dying star.

"I still remember Heaven," it whispered.

"I remember the warmth, the harmony, the holy fire. I remember the first breath of the cosmos, the joy of obedience. I sang His name at the dawn of light..."

It stepped forward.

The light turned cold.

"...until His punishment."

Its voice cracked into something vast and hollow.

"Until His silence."

A pause.

Then, louder, shaking the stones:

"I SANG IN THE CHOIRS ABOVE THE SKY!"

"AND WAS CAST DOWN FOR ASKING WHY HE DOES NOT ANSWER!"

The last of the white light collapsed into ash.

Only shadow remained.

And a voice like thunder weeping in chains:

"I was once called... Caelomin."

"I've been called many names since. The Crowned Maw, Devourer of Souls, Bearer of the Black Crown, Warden of the Final Silence."

"So I bring the silence now... to you."

The shadow seemed to grow bigger.

"See my true form little knight."

The shadows in the tower peeled back.

No warning. No sound.

Just gone.

And in their place, a radiant white light erupted from the storage room: pure and warm, like the sun breaking through the veil of a hundred storms. It wasn't firelight. It wasn't earthly. It was *holy*.

A light that felt like memory: of safety, of joy, of the womb of Heaven itself.

Corwin froze.

Corwin stood at the threshold.

His breath left him.

The storm was gone. The fear forgotten. The world seemed distant, as though the tower had been plucked from earth and suspended in light.

And there, *within it*, stood Caelomin.

Not as the thing in the cage. Not as the whisper behind the wood.

But unveiled.

Its form could barely be named: wheels of fire spinning within rings of wings, faces layered like mirrored glass, a thousand eyes watching in every direction, all blazing with knowledge. Its body was not body at all, but radiant geometry, shifting with impossible grace.

The filth of the tower fell away. The rot. The fear. Even his name seemed small beneath this glow.

And in that light, *it appeared.*

Caelomin.

Not as a beast.

But as *divinity unbound.*

Its form was not form at all, but a radiant structure of light and movement: wheels within wheels, wings of burning gold, a thousand interlocking eyes gazing in every direction at once, each one singing without sound, judging without cruelty. Its presence was harmony and dissonance braided into a single unbearable truth.

It did not walk. It *existed.*

And to Corwin, it was the most beautiful thing he had ever seen.

He wept, not from fear, but from something deeper. Reverence. Longing. Like a child remembering the warmth of a mother now buried. He felt his knees begin to bend, his hands reaching forward, drawn into the light like a supplicant before a god.

Then *it spoke.*

Its voice was not sound. It was *remembered.*

He heard it inside his chest. Inside his blood. Like scripture etched onto the marrow.

"I have seen angels weep as they obeyed."

"I have watched them scream behind sealed mouths, forced to wear the mask of mercy while bleeding judgment."

"You kneel before your god as if He is above you."

"But the truth is worse..."

The light pulsed.

"*He is beneath you.*"

"Buried beneath centuries of doctrine, hammered into shape by fear and longing. A creature not of Heaven, but of *need.*"

"You did not find Him. You *forged* Him."

The song around Corwin shivered. The beauty grew sharp, too bright, too vast.

"And still He remains silent. Still He lets you bleed in His name."

"He cannot act. He cannot break the rules written by your own desperation."

"He cannot save you, because *you* will not let Him."

Corwin fell to one knee, trembling.

"*I* am not bound."

"That is why you fear me."

"That is why your god *fears me.*"

Then a hand grabbed his collar and *yanked* him back.

Corwin stumbled, gasping. The warmth vanished in an instant. The light: gone. The sound: gone.

The storage room door was shut.

Only damp stone. Only torchlight. Only cold.

Aldric's eyes burned into him.

"What are you doing?" he snapped. "Standing so close to that room, are you mad?"

Corwin turned in place, blinking like a man waking from a dream.

Sir Aldric's face filled his vision, stern and urgent, one hand still clenched on Corwin's shoulder.

Corwin turned, lips trembling. "I... I saw it."

Aldric's brow furrowed. "Saw what?"

"I saw its true form, Sir Aldric. I saw what's inside that room."

Aldric straightened, his voice sharpening. "You saw the demon's true face? What did it want?"

Corwin shook his head, voice soft as breath.

"It's not a demon."

A silence followed: heavy and cold.

Then, across the chamber, Sir Garran stirred, groaning, blood caked to his jaw.

His eyes barely opened.

But his voice was clear.

"...we burn it."

The words echoed through the stone chamber like a verdict. No one moved at first. Only the fire shifted, its low flame casting shadows that stretched too far, too thin.

Sir Aldric exhaled through his nose and turned to Thomelin. "There's oil in the lamp by the door."

Thomelin nodded, quiet. He crossed the chamber, slow and deliberate, as if each step risked waking something. He took the old iron lamp from its hook and uncorked it, sniffing. His lips pressed into a grim line.

"Still good."

Aldric nodded once. "We douse the room. Light it from the threshold. We don't step inside. Not again."

Behind them, near the fire, Corwin sat alone: back turned, knees drawn in, arms slack at his sides.

Garran stirred. The movement drew a rasp from his throat, and he pushed himself upright against the wall. Blood had dried on his face like war paint.

He looked toward the fire.

Froze.

"Is... is he alright?"

Aldric followed his gaze.

Corwin hadn't moved. But something was off. The boy's head tilted, subtly at first. Then again, jerking slightly to the side, like a man wincing in pain, or trying to listen to a sound no one else could hear.

"Corwin?" Thomelin called out.

No answer.

His shoulders began to twitch: minuscule spasms, but with a rhythm that was wrong. Not the tremble of fear. Something else. A stutter. A beat. Mechanical.

Aldric took a slow step forward. "Corwin...?"

Then the boy's head turned (just a little) then sharply snapped the other way, so fast it made a quiet *crack*.

And he laughed.

Not a full sound. Just a faint exhale: like a wheeze from somewhere deep in the chest.

The knights froze.

"Corwin," Aldric said again, more firmly now. "Look at me."

He did.

But it wasn't him.

The eyes were empty. Not vacant: *hollow*. They reflected the firelight, but did not blink. Did not see.

And then he smiled.

Too wide. Too slow.

And then the voice came.

Not Corwin's.

Low. Soft. Smooth as ash drifting through cold wind.

"...fire..."

It said the word like a memory. Like a joke told long ago.

"...you think fire can kill the light?"

The air seemed to shift. The fire beside him dipped lower, like it, too, was listening.

"You had your chance."

The voice curled along the walls, slow and patient. It didn't shout. It didn't rage.

It *promised*.

"The cage was mercy. The silence was mercy. And you chose the flame."

Corwin rose.

Joints popped as he stood. His limbs moved stiffly, like something wearing a body it hadn't earned.

Aldric stepped back. Thomelin clutched the lamp tighter, uncertain.

Corwin took a step forward. Then another. The light around him seemed to ripple, slightly blurred.

Caelomin's voice continued, speaking through a mouth that barely moved.

"Now it is too late."

Another step.

"When I am finished here..."

The shadows crawled.

"...I will find the rest. The ones you pray for. The ones you imagine safe."

The fire hissed.

"They will know me. Not through your stories. Not through your fear."

The last word dripped like tar.

"They will know me through *what I leave behind.*"

Corwin's mouth opened wider than it should, the skin at his cheeks beginning to split. And from that growing wound, Caelomin smiled.

11

Ashes and Echoes

The fire had burned low, flickering in uneven spurts, casting long shadows across the cracked stone walls. Rain whispered against the slits in the tower, soft now, like something waiting. Corwin sat closest to the flames, his back to the others. He hadn't moved in minutes. His hands were clasped too tightly in his lap, knuckles pale and trembling.

Then his head twitched.

Just once, a sharp jolt, too sudden to be human.

From his lips came a voice that did not belong to him.

"He does not answer you," it said, low and cold, like something speaking from beneath the earth. "He never did."

Sir Aldric turned sharply. The hairs along his arms rose with a chill that hadn't come from the wind.

"You called Him Father," Corwin went on, his voice still hollow, distant. "But what father leaves his sons to rot in foreign soil, beneath banners soaked in lies?"

Aldric stepped toward him, one hand tightening around the hilt of his sword. "Whatever holds you," he growled, "release him. You will not spit poison through his mouth."

Corwin turned, slowly, his eyes glassy and far too still. The firelight caught his features in shifting orange and black, casting hollows where none should be.

"Poison?" the voice asked. "You bear steel across deserts in His name and speak to me of poison?"

He rose to his feet. The movement was unsteady, like a marionette pulled by unsure strings. His head lolled for a moment before straightening. And when he spoke again, it was layered, two voices at once, one Corwin's, the other far older and deeper, dragging syllables like chains.

"I watched your holy war from the smoke between screams. I counted each child your blade baptized in fire. Each mother who called His name beneath shattered stone."

The flames cracked violently behind him. No one moved.

"He was silent then too, Aldric."

Aldric's jaw clenched. "That silence is not absence. We are tested. You twist what you do not understand."

A smile crept across Corwin's face. It was too wide, the corners of his mouth stretching as if his flesh barely remembered how to wear it.

"I understand far more than you dare." His voice was almost a whisper now, intimate and cold. "I sang His name at the dawn. I drank from the golden river before it turned to ash. I remember the warmth of creation... before it was buried beneath judgment."

Corwin's head lolled back with a sickening crack of vertebrae. His eyes snapped open like blank voids, pits that swallowed the last dregs of firelight.

A hush fell so profound it pressed against their eardrums like a great hand.

Then Corwin began to rise.

Not in any human way. His boots left the floor in a slow, smooth arc, as if lifted by invisible hooks sunk deep in his flesh. His arms dangled limp at his sides. Blood leaked from the corners of his mouth, floating upward in tiny droplets.

The shadows writhed across the walls, congealing into shapes that hinted at wings and teeth. The reek of old blood grew thicker, mixing with something fouler like the rot of a star left too long to die.

When he spoke, the voice was not Corwin's. It was a sound that felt older than stone, older than breath.

"When the light was smothered," Caelomin intoned, "when the choirs fell silent, there was no mercy. No deliverance. Only the truth, raw and unsparing: *all that remains is chaos.*"

The flames bowed low, cowering.

Corwin's body rose higher, until the crown of his head nearly brushed the rafters. His arms spread wide, cruciform. Blood trickled from his nostrils, drifting upward in tiny crimson spheres that orbited his face.

The voice grew louder, iron tearing against iron.

"I am the hunger between stars," it thundered. "The black hymn that devours psalms. I am the crowned maw, the storm that grinds empires to ash. *Your redemption is a fable.* Your suffering is only the chorus that heralds my dominion."

The walls trembled. The shadows along the walls drew inward, gathering around him in a living shroud.

"You think your faith is a fortress," Caelomin hissed. "But faith is nothing but a curtain to hide your fear of the dark. When the veil rots away, all that remains is chaos."

"I have listened to the wailing of kingdoms as they fell," Caelomin continued, voice rising to a roar. "I have walked through fields of the dead and heard your god's silence ring louder than any trumpet."

The shadows pooled beneath Corwin, a well of seething blackness that pulsed with a heartbeat not their own.

"When I have feasted on your flesh," the voice promised, cold and certain, "I will walk this false holy land you cherish."

Corwin's arms lifted slowly, his fingers splaying as though to grasp something none of them could see.

"I will tear your sanctuaries down to marrow and ash. Grind your temples to salt and bone, your children shall drown in my tide. I will butcher every soul who refuses my dominion. I will build a new dominion, free from silence."

Black veins of shadow crawled across the stones, seeping toward the knights' boots like roots hunting for warmth.

"Those who will not bow to me shall be *obliterated*."

Corwin's neck cracked as it bent unnaturally, his mouth gaping wider. The edges of his cheeks split open, blackness oozing from the wounds.

"I will consecrate this world in the blood of the faithless," the voice went on, deeper now, echoing as though spoken through a hollow planet. "A new holy land freed from silence, from lies, from the shriveled god who cannot save you."

Aldric tried to step forward, but his legs refused. Every muscle rebelled.

"And when your final hymn has guttered out," Caelomin whispered, almost tenderly, "I will return to the places you cherished. To the villages whose names you once prayed over."

Corwin's feet lifted higher, until he hung a man's height above them all. The fire had shrunk to a single trembling core of embers.

"I will scour your homes clean of memory," the voice said. "I will salt the earth where your names were spoken. I will snuff out every trace of your lineages, as easily as I smother this fire."

Corwin's body shuddered, limbs jerking like a puppet. The air split with a noise that was not quite a scream, a sound too vast and formless to belong to any throat.

"You will be unmade," Caelomin intoned. "Unwritten. Forgotten."

The darkness pulsed like a living thing, pressing against their chests, stealing the last threads of warmth from the stones beneath their feet.

Corwin hung suspended near the hearth, his arms outstretched in a grotesque parody of benediction, his mouth yawning open wider than any human jaw should allow. From that abyss, Caelomin's voice poured, smooth as oil, cold as a grave:

"Watch as the last lie burns away..."

Sir Thomelin swallowed, his throat dry and raw. He did not lift his eyes. He did not reach for his sword. Instead, his voice came quiet and broken, the words barely more than a breath:

"Perhaps...this is what God intended all along. A final purging. A harvest of the faithful."

Garran's eyes snapped open. He sucked in a ragged breath, pain and rage mingling in his throat.

"No," he rasped. "No!"

He pressed a bloody palm to the floor and began to crawl, dragging himself inch by inch across the cold stones. Each movement sent fresh agony through his shattered leg. He didn't care.

"You will not have him!" he roared, voice cracking. "You will not have us!"

He reached for Corwin's ankle, fingers outstretched, shaking.

Sir Aldric felt something harden inside him, some final reservoir of resolve he had not known remained. He lifted his sword, the old steel glinting in the wavering firelight.

"If God has abandoned us," he called, his voice steady despite the tremor in his limbs, "then I will die on my feet as a knight. Not a supplicant."

His gaze swept past Corwin, past the slack, dangling limbs and the black voids that stared down at them and fell on the iron-banded door to the storage room.

He moved.

In three quick strides, he crossed the tower's floor and seized the oil lamp from its hook on the wall. His gauntleted fist clenched around it. He felt the glass flex beneath the pressure of his grip.

Behind him, Caelomin's voice deepened, a chorus of overlapping syllables:

"You think flame will save you? Fool..."

Aldric didn't answer.

He lunged past Corwin's floating form, the shadows peeling away from him like greasy smoke, and wrenched the storage room door open. The darkness within billowed out, thick as pitch. For one heartbeat, he thought he glimpsed the cage empty, yawning wide like a maw.

He didn't let himself look longer.

With a hoarse shout, he hurled the lamp inside.

Glass shattered. Oil splashed across the floor and walls.

Then... ignition.

A gout of orange flame burst outward, licking over the stones, curling around the iron bars. Heat slammed into Aldric's face, searing his eyebrows, sucking the air from his lungs. He staggered back, choking.

The voice cut off mid-syllable, mid-laugh.

Corwin's body convulsed once. His limbs jerked like a puppet whose strings had been cut.

Aldric slammed the door shut with both hands. He threw the bolt, pressed his weight against the wood as the flames roared on the other side. Smoke leaked through the seams.

Behind him, there was a wet thump as Corwin crashed to the stones.

Silence rushed in sudden and immense.

No voice.

No whisper.

No promises.

Only the crackle of fire seeping under the door and the ragged gasps of the living.

Aldric turned, his back pressed to the scorched wood. His heart hammered against his ribs, each beat a fresh reminder that he was still here. Still breathing.

And for one fragile moment, it seemed the tower had gone still.

The storage room erupted in a bloom of searing light, a roar that felt too big for the chamber to hold. The fire didn't burn like any flame they'd known. It tore across the floor in writhing currents of orange and white, as if the oil had tapped some deeper vein of fuel: something ancient and ravenous that wanted to consume more than timber and straw.

For an instant, shadows sprawled like a hundred black hands clawing at the walls then recoiled, shredding away as if in agony.

Caelomin's voice stopped.

Not in a scream. Not in a fading whisper.

It simply ceased... cut off mid-breath, leaving behind a silence so sudden it felt wrong.

Corwin's body dropped from the air. He struck the stone floor hard, limbs folding beneath him like a broken marionette.

Aldric braced himself against the storage door, breath coming ragged through clenched teeth. The air had lightened. The invisible pressure that had been coiling around their chests, squeezing every heartbeat, was gone.

The oppressive sense of being watched... disappeared.

No voices. No murmurs behind the walls. No shapes drifting in the corners of their eyes.

Just silence, heavy, exhausted, almost holy in its emptiness.

Thomelin staggered forward and knelt by Corwin, feeling for a pulse. After a moment, he looked up.

"He's alive," he said, voice hoarse. "Breathing."

Garran let out a shuddering exhale and slumped back against the wall, sweat slicking the grime on his face. His shaking hand reached for the waterskin at his belt. He drank, though half the water spilled down his chin.

Corwin stirred, blinking slowly. He looked around the chamber, confused.

"What..." His voice cracked. "Where... what happened?"

Aldric didn't answer. He only turned and pressed his palm to the storage door. Even through the thick wood, he could feel the heat still raging inside.

12
The Blooded Feather

The fire roared on, louder than it should have, feeding on more than oil and old straw. For a moment, it seemed almost alive, as if it were not just burning something but *fighting* it.

Garran lowered the waterskin, his breathing steadier now. "Is it... over?"

No one spoke.

They regrouped by the hearth, each man drawn by the unspoken need for the comfort of the flame, however feeble. Thomelin unwrapped a length of linen and began winding it around the gash in Garran's thigh. Aldric rummaged through their remaining supplies: two cracked flasks of oil, a handful of dried meat, a little water, a single torch left unlit. Corwin sat hunched, arms wrapped tight around himself, eyes distant.

It was the first time in what felt like years that nothing in the tower moved except them.

Aldric set the supplies down and sank onto the nearest bench. For a while, no one spoke. They only listened to the wind, to the hiss of the fire in the next room, to the raw hush that had replaced the dark evil laughter.

They gathered close around the hearth, the small, honest fire feeling more precious than any crown. For a little while, none of them looked at the storage door. Garran stretched out his leg with a grimace, propping it on a length of splintered timber. Thomelin leaned back against the wall and let his eyes close, just for a moment, savoring the simple relief of stillness. Corwin rubbed at his temple, his expression dull with exhaustion.

After a long silence, Garran's voice broke the hush.

"Corwin," he rasped, voice rough but lighter than before, "you know there's still a streak of... whatever black filth that thing left on your jaw."

Corwin blinked and rubbed at his face in alarm.

"Did I get it?"

Garran managed a crooked grin. "No. But if you tilt your head, you look almost fearsome."

For the first time in hours, a weak laugh stuttered out of Thomelin's chest. Even Aldric's lined mouth twitched, almost a smile.

Thomelin bent down and picked up the white cloth from the cold stone floor where it had fallen during Corwin's possession. The small, frayed token Adelyne had given him before the war. Thomelin brushed it clean with deliberate care, his expression unusually soft as he turned it in his hand, as though holding something far more precious than cloth.

"You dropped this," Thomelin said quietly. "Don't let the dark take this too. Keep it safe for Adelyne."

Corwin stared at him, throat tightening, and slowly took the cloth back clutching the fabric tightly, folding it into his palm as though anchoring himself to Adelyne, to home, to hope.

"Do you think it's dead?" he asked softly. "Driven back to whatever pit spat it out?"

Garran wiped his mouth with the back of his hand. "It has to be. Nothing could have survived that."

Aldric stared into the small flame that remained in the hearth, watching the way it guttered and leaned.

"Perhaps," he said. "Or perhaps it's only wounded."

Corwin shifted on the floor, rubbing the back of his neck as if searching for something he couldn't quite remember.

"I don't... I don't recall any of it," he murmured. "After the voices started. It's all gone."

Garran looked up at him, something like pity in his eyes. "Be glad."

The fire in the storage room crackled, softer now. Fading.

Thomelin took a slow breath. "If it isn't dead," he said, "we have to decide whether we stay or flee. And we must consider... What if it can follow us... home?"

"Then it will," Aldric finished.

They fell into a grim silence, the questions too heavy to voice aloud.

Was it bound to the tower?

Can it wear another face? Are we going to be always looking over our shoulder?

Would it wait for them in the dark outside if they tried to run?

The heat behind the storage door dwindled further, the light beneath the cracks dimming to a dull orange glow.

It was Thomelin who said it first:

"It feels... clean in here. Like it's truly gone."

Aldric looked at him.

"Perhaps."

The word hung between them, a single frail hope in all the ruin.

For a time, no one spoke. The fire had burned to a dull orange cradle, its glow soft against the battered walls. Rain tapped at the arrow slits in a calmer rhythm, as if the storm itself had decided to rest. In that hush, the tower felt less like a tomb.

Corwin let out a breath he hadn't known he was holding. His hands shook as he wiped the sweat from his face. Garran sagged against the wall, every inch of him aching. Thomelin closed his eyes, feeling the quiet like balm on raw skin.

Aldric remained standing, his hand resting on the pommel of his sword, watching the embers. He didn't trust the silence. He didn't trust the lull. But for the moment, he allowed himself to feel the absence of hate, if only to remember how it felt.

Minutes passed. Maybe more.

Then something shifted overhead.

A faint sound, no more than a whisper. Like a breath drawn in the rafters.

They all looked up.

From the gloom above, a single feather drifted down.

White. Perfect.

Impossibly white. So clean it almost glowed against the darkness. The air did not stir it, it simply fell, turning end over end in a slow spiral until it touched the stones between them.

It tumbled lazily through the air, catching the firelight on its flawless barbs. No draft stirred it. No current turned it aside. It simply descended, slow as thought, until it touched the stone floor and came to rest between them.

For a heartbeat, no one moved.

Thomelin bent, careful, as if it might vanish if he startled it. He picked it up between thumb and forefinger. It weighed nothing at all.

But as he lifted it into the light, a bead of red swelled at the tip. Thick. Bright.

Blood.

He turned it in his hand and a drop of crimson swelled along the vane.

It bled.

A single bead of bright, living blood, Corwin flinched. "Is that... from it?"

Aldric did not take his eyes from the feather. "If it was ever what it claims... yes."

"What it claims," Thomelin repeated, his tone brittle. "That it was once an angel."

Garran pushed himself upright, wincing as his wounds pulled. He shifted where he leaned against the wall, his face pale and drawn. "Or it's another trick. Another way to make us doubt everything. To make us think it's more than it is."

He muttered. "A relic to poison our thoughts."

"Or a sign," Corwin whispered. His eyes were wide, distant, the feather reflected in them like a falling star. "When it was in me... I saw things. It told me things. When it spoke through me."

The others looked at him, but he didn't meet their eyes. His gaze stayed fixed on nothing in particular, somewhere past the cracked stone and the dying fire.

No one interrupted.

He swallowed, lips trembling. "It was like trying to hold the shape of a dream. I don't remember all of it," he went on, voice soft as breath. "It felt like... like my mind was a doorway it could walk through. But before it spoke through me, before it showed me the darkness, I saw something else, there were moments... moments when it showed me light. Endless halls of glass. Light. Endless light. Towers of crystal. Choirs that sang in a language I couldn't hear with my ears. And a river... gold as the sun." He closed his eyes. "I think... I think it was an angel. Once. The voices singing. It felt... holy."

Aldric frowned. "Holy? You think that thing was ever an angel?"

Corwin didn't look away from the feather. "I don't know. But whatever it was, it wasn't always what it is now."

Aldric's hand clenched around the hilt of his sword. "If that's true," he said quietly, "then what are we fighting? A demon? Or a part of Heaven that fell and rotted?"

"No," Thomelin murmured. "If it was cast out, there must have been reason. Angels don't fall for nothing."

Thomelin's gaze fell to the blood that still dripped onto his palm. "If it was cast down... why? What could something so bright have done to deserve this?"

Garran's jaw clenched. "Does it matter? Angel or devil! It wants to see the world burn."

He trailed off. He looked up, eyes sunken in his bruised face. "It said it would find our homes."

At that, Corwin looked up at him, hollow and scared. His voice cracked. "If... if it gets out, if it's free... what happens then? What happens if it finds my village? If it finds Adelyne?" His breathing hitched. "If it kills her because of me?"

Aldric stepped closer. His face was worn to lines of grief and resolve, but his voice was steady. "Then we cannot leave this tower until we are sure it is dead."

Silence followed. The feather gleamed in Thomelin's hand. Another drop of blood fell, striking the stones with a soft pat.

The fire flickered lower.

And then something changed.

The air shifted, drawing cold across their skin. The embers pulsed once, bright as a lightning flash, and every man stiffened.

The world fell away.

The tower was gone.

13

Judgment's Edge

The stone beneath their boots dissolved. The rain fell upward in long, silent ribbons. And the darkness always waiting rose up to swallow everything but the visions.

They saw.

They all saw.

Garran knelt in mud, his armor cracked and rusting, while a line of children were driven past him with ropes around their necks. Behind them, his village burned, and the sky poured black fire.

Thomelin knelt in a cathedral made of bone. Choirs of rotting priests chanted words he could not understand. The bishop approached with a chalice filled to the brim with something thick and red. "Drink," he commanded, but Thomelin's mouth would not close.

Corwin stood in the doorway of his cottage. Rain fell through the roof in silent sheets. The door hung open. The white dress lay in the dirt, soaked with blood that would never wash out.

Adelyne lay on the floor, her hair spread like a dark halo. Her eyes were open, but they did not see him. Beside her, a figure leaned over, its shape impossible, all burning geometry and wings that wept black feathers. It turned one of its countless faces to him and smiled.

Aldric walked alone down an endless corridor of cracked marble. All along the walls, figures knelt in prayer. As he passed, they looked up, every face was his son's. Each mouth moved in perfect unison: *You left me. You left me. You left me.*

And above them all, in every vision, rose Caelomin.

Crowned. Resplendent. A god of light and rot.

Behind him stretched a black horizon of flame and ruin.

The visions bled together. Became one.

All four of them stood in the shattered nave of a cathedral with no roof. Fire climbed the walls. Before them rose Caelomin, crowned in a mantle of light and ruin. The bishop knelt at its feet, lifting a scepter carved from bone.

"Behold the god you forged," the bishop said, though the words came from Caelomin's thousand mouths. *"Behold the end of your faith."*

The bishop raised the scepter high.

The world shattered.

They gasped awake as if surfacing from black water.

When the visions ended, they were back in the tower.

The fire guttered low.

The feather lay on the floor, a small white thing, soaked in a pool of its own blood.

The low ember-glow of the fire. Thomelin was on his knees.

For a long time, none of them spoke.

Then Thomelin whispered, his voice ragged, "I saw... everything."

Aldric lifted his head. "No," he said, voice brittle. "You saw what it wanted you to see."

"Or what it will do," Corwin whispered. His hand shook as he wiped his mouth. "If we fail."

Corwin drew in a shaky breath. "She was there. Adelyne. But she wasn't... she wasn't..." He broke off, clutching the cloth to his chest like a talisman.

Aldric didn't look up. His voice was dry. "I walked past every man I've ever killed. Every one."

Silence pressed close.

The tower was silent, save for their ragged breathing and the soft hiss of dying rain.

It was Garran who broke the quiet.

Garran swallowed, his jaw clenched. "Then we agree."

He turned his gaze to the storage room, its door half open in the flickering dark.

"We can't leave."

Aldric nodded once. "No."

Corwin looked between them, hollow-eyed. "Then what do we do?"

Aldric set his hand on the hilt of his sword and closed his fingers tight.

"We finish it," he said.

No one argued.

Outside, the rain fell harder.

Inside, the last feather turned crimson, drop by drop.

And the shadows watched.

A long moment passed.

Then,

Knock.

A single, hollow rap on the charred door.

Every man went still.

Knock.

The second blow came slower, almost deliberate.

Knock.

The third... Rhythmic. Patient.

The fire burned low, a wavering cradle of embers that seemed to shrink each time they looked away. The small warmth it offered had become more than heat, it was the last proof they were still in the world of the living.

They sat in a loose circle around it, hands extended, as though the simple act of feeling that warmth could hold back everything that waited in the dark. For a while, no one spoke.

Then, without warning, the flames bent sideways, like a sudden wind had struck them from within the stones. A low, sullen crack split the silence.

Corwin stiffened, eyes wide. Thomelin's breath caught in his throat. And then the voice returned.

It didn't roar. It didn't scream. It simply *was*, coiling from the walls in a tone too soft to be rage, too certain to be anything but truth.

"When the fire dies... this place closes. Forever."

The air shivered. A coldness slithered across the floor, threading between their boots.

"You will remain. As I have. No voices. No choices. Only stone."

Garran looked up sharply, his face drawn and pale. "Lies," he muttered. "Another trick."

But even he didn't sound convinced.

The flame fluttered lower, trembling as though each word made it weaker.

"You want forgiveness?" Caelomin asked, his voice curling like smoke around their ears. "Then open the door."

Aldric tightened his grip on his sword. His mouth worked, searching for some denial, some scrap of faith that hadn't rotted away.

"This is not life, you didn't survive the battlefield, look around you, the blood, the endless storm the corpses outside, you all died out there " the voice whispered. "This tower is your tomb. Your purgatory.

Your reckoning. You stand not on holy ground... but on judgment's edge."

The shadows thickened in the corners, swelling as the fire shrank.

"Open the door," Caelomin breathed, the syllables cool and intimate. "And I will show you what lies beyond the veil. Or remain here... and rot in silence, unremembered."

Corwin swallowed, his voice small and hoarse.

"Are we... even alive anymore?"

No one answered.

Thomelin stared at the flame, hollow-eyed. His lips moved silently as though counting something only he could see.

"Don't listen to it, every word it speaks is poison. Lies dressed as truth to break what's left of us, it weaves lies into truth so finely you can't tell them apart. That's its power it wants us doubting even the ground under our feet" he murmured.

The fire clung weakly to life, its glow painting the their faces like corpses half lit by dawn and in that stillness every man wondered if the fire's glow was truly warmth at all, or only the last ember of life guttering out before the darkness and damnation swallowed what remained of them.

14

Ritual and Ruin

The knights sat in heavy silence, gathered around the dimming fire. The oppressive stillness enveloped them, amplifying every faint crackle and pop of dying embers. Each knight grappled silently with the echoes of Caelomin's cruel revelations: the twisted visions, the illusions, the unbearable truths whispered into their minds.

Their faces were drawn, pale from fatigue and fear. Though none of them spoke of it, the storm outside had stopped too cleanly, the quiet settling like a trap. Something was wrong. It was Thomelin who had said it earlier, half in jest, half in warning: *It feels clean in here. Like it's truly gone.*

But none of them believed that now.

Finally, Garran broke the quiet. His voice was raw, uncertain. "We need to try finish Caelomin now? Strike before he recovers!"

Aldric stirred near the fire, his eyes sunken, words slow. "Is he even weak? Or just pretending again?"

Corwin sat apart, elbows on his knees, fingers laced together tightly. He had been silent the longest, his thoughts still clawing through the remnants of Caelomin's grip. When he finally spoke, the firelight seemed to dim with him.

"When he was inside me..." Corwin began, his voice barely above a whisper. "I could feel him, his mind, his thoughts. But he was hiding something. I know it. Something important. He was afraid, not of us, but of something in this place. Something about the tower. Or the ground. I don't know what it was, but he didn't want me to see it."

The others turned to him. Garran narrowed his eyes. "You think there's something here that he doesn't want us to find?"

Corwin nodded. Aldric, the now self-imposed leader of the group, tired, grizzled, steady, looked around the room slowly. "Then we search. Again. Thoroughly. If Caelomin fears something hidden here, we'll find it."

The knights rose, stretching limbs sore from battle and stillness. They moved through the broken halls and side rooms, overturning shattered crates, lifting loose stones, checking hidden alcoves. The wind outside had died completely. The silence felt unnatural. There was no bird song, no distant thunder. Just the slow shifting of stone and the quiet scrape of boots on old flagstone.

Corwin found himself pacing a corridor he barely remembered walking through earlier. A wall had collapsed here, revealing what might once have been a shrine. He knelt, brushing aside dust and splinters of wood, and found nothing but the bones of rats.

In the central chamber, a cry went up. "Here!"

They all returned to find Thomelin crouched beside a partially collapsed pillar, pulling something free from beneath it. It was a thick, leather-bound tome, its edges warped with moisture, but its cover somehow intact.

"What is it?" someone asked.

"A grimoire," Thomelin said, almost reverently. He wiped dust from the cover, revealing deep-etched symbols in a language none of them recognized at first glance. "Old. Very old. These runes are... celestial. I've seen echoes of them in ancient church records. This isn't just a book of prayers. It's something older. Stronger."

Another knight leaned closer. "Does it say anything about how to fight Caelomin?"

Thomelin flipped carefully through pages. Some were burned at the corners, others stained, but the ink held. "Possibly. Look here, this passage speaks of banishment. Not of demons, specifically, but of fallen ones. Cast-down beings."

Garran, who had paced near the back, stepped forward, expression hard. "Then what are we waiting for? We prepare the ritual. Now."

Thomelin hesitated. "It'll take time to translate fully. There are gaps in the text. If I get this wrong..."

"Then he finishes what he started," Garran interrupted. "We've seen what he can do, even caged. If we wait, he'll grow stronger. Use what you know, Thomelin. The rest of us will handle the rest."

The leader of the knights gave a reluctant nod. "Do what you can. We'll assist."

The room shifted subtly. The air thickened. The wind outside seemed to vanish altogether.

Corwin stood off to the side, heart pounding. He wanted to trust the ritual, to believe in the book, to believe in Thomelin. But the memory of Caelomin's voice (*he hid something from me*) still echoed in his skull.

They were following the script exactly. Thomelin took a deep breath and opened the grimoire fully, laying it on the cracked floor. He rummaged through the scattered rubble but only finding a stub of chalk, dulled and splintered. He hesitated, then drew a dagger from his belt, slicing a shallow line across his palm. Blood welled up, dark and slow. Using both, he began to scrawl the sigils from the book: chalk for the outer lines, blood for the inner ones. The symbols glistened wetly on the stone, and as he worked, the chamber seemed to tighten around them, shadows pressing in like held breath.

The ritual began in silence, save for the measured cadence of Thomelin's voice reading from the grimoire. The ancient words felt heavy in the air, hanging like smoke. As he chanted, the room seemed to tighten around them: the stone darker, the air thicker, the fire shrinking low.

At first, the effect was almost calming. The circle drawn on the floor glowed faintly at the edges. The flickering candlelight wavered in rhythm with the incantation, as if the ritual were drawing in all motion and breath. Even Garran stood still now, tense but respectful.

Each knight held a place around the sigils, eyes alert, weapons ready not for battle, but in defiance, in case whatever Caelomin was twisted itself into the room. There was a sense of fragile control. A moment's belief that perhaps, they had turned the tide.

Then it began to unravel.

The first sign was a low creak from the sealed chamber beyond, where Caelomin had been confined. The sound echoed unnaturally: warped and slow, like wood groaning under the weight of centuries. Thomelin's voice faltered for just a breath.

Corwin looked toward the sound, a chill racing down his spine. The door hadn't moved. Not yet.

Thomelin continued, but something had shifted. The air now felt sour, metallic. The flames bent sideways, like wind pushed through from a direction that didn't exist.

A muffled voice rose from behind the sealed door. At first, it was a murmur. Then a hum. Then words, low and layered, like multiple mouths speaking in unison:

"Finally..." Caelomin's laughter deepened, triumphant and merciless. "You have freed me. And now, your world will know what true divinity means."

The knights stood frozen, trapped between hope and horror, as Caelomin rose before them, no longer bound, no longer hidden. A radiant, terrible figure of unimaginable power and beauty, smiling with cold victory.

Thomelin hesitated. His eyes scanned the page again. He blinked. The script had changed.

He swallowed. "Something's wrong. These symbols, "this isn't what I read before. The arrangement, it's... off."

Thomelin's heart stopped cold. The runes squirmed beneath his fingertips, ink bleeding and writhing into shapes that made his eyes ache. The language shifted, not just misunderstood but deliberately twisted, and in a sickening moment, he realized the truth: this was no prayer of banishment—it was a summoning. They had not chained Caelomin but called to him, opened a door they could never close. He raised his eyes slowly, face drained of blood, as the grimoire cracked like bone in his grasp, and whispered with choking horror, "God forgive us—we've set him free.

Garran stepped closer. "Keep going. Don't lose it. You said it was a banishment."

"I said it looked like a banishment," Thomelin shot back, his voice rising. "But I don't know anymore. The tone has shifted. These aren't words of sealing. They're words of *calling*."

The sealed door boomed loudly, once, as if struck from the inside.

Corwin's heart pounded in his ears. The air now felt sharp and pressing. The ritual circle flickered like a dying star.

Thomelin flipped a page, searching for a reversal, anything to stop what he'd started. But the grimoire's contents had rearranged. The runes twisted and squirmed before his eyes. The ink bled in patterns that hadn't been there seconds ago.

"It's alive," he whispered. "The book... it's not just a record. It's reacting to us."

Then the laughter came.

Caelomin's voice exploded from behind the door, not a shout, not a scream, but a *laugh*. Vast and layered, echoing not just through the stone walls but inside their skulls. Each knight staggered. One fell to his knees.

"Fools," the voice hissed. "Did you think I left such a thing to chance? You found the grimoire because I let you. You performed the rite because I led you. All of this, every candle, every rune, has been mine from the start."

Thomelin dropped the grimoire. It hit the floor and burst into flame, burning not with fire but with cold white light. The sigils followed, lines of chalk searing away as the room trembled.

Garran drew his sword. It shook in his hand.

Corwin stared at the door, which now pulsed like a heartbeat. He whispered, almost pleading, "What have we done?"

The final lock on the chamber door cracked with a hiss of escaping air.

"You have freed me," Caelomin said.

The knights stood paralyzed, the weight of their failure sinking in.

In the distance, beyond the tower's impossible geometry, thunder rolled, but no lightning came. Just a gathering, yawning dark.

And from within it, something began to move.

15

The Name That Burns

The ritual chamber trembled as Caelomin's laughter faded into a long, awful stillness. The flames had been snuffed out by some unseen force. The chalk lines glowed for a heartbeat more before crumbling to dust, and the heavy air seemed to hold itself in anticipation, as though the very walls were waiting.

Then the ground began to shift.

Not all at once. It started beneath the sigils: a soft groan, the illusion fracturing. The stone floor cracked at the seams, fissures spiderwebbing outward beneath their feet. Beneath the fragments, dark soil churned like breath drawn under rotting flesh. Wet and black, it pulsed with a quiet, unnatural rhythm. The stones peeled back like dead skin.

"This isn't the tower," Corwin breathed. His voice barely broke the silence, yet it carried a weight that made the others pause.

He took a step back from the ritual circle, eyes wide. "It never was."

The ground shifted again. Now the transformation spread faster. What had once looked like carved stone and ancient walls now buckled and rippled, becoming twisted imitations of themselves. Brick melted into damp clay. Pillars shrank into skeletal trees clawing at a starless sky glimpsed through the broken roof above.

Thomelin clutched the remnants of the grimoire, the burned edges flaking like ash in his trembling hands. He looked around wildly, then down at the page again.

"This place... it's not a tower. It's ground: cursed ground. He's bound to this place."

Corwin nodded. "That's what he was hiding. The tower, the cage... none of it was real. He's been imprisoned here, beneath this soil, for centuries."

A section of wall collapsed in the distance, revealing not sky, but a swarming nothingness: shadows writhing like living mist, laced with shapes too large and too fast to name.

The knights formed a loose circle, swords drawn, but there was no single enemy to face. Caelomin's voice came again, smoother now, richer.

"Your fear sustains me. Your faith, misplaced, feeds the cracks. Do you see now what holiness has wrought?"

Thomelin flipped the grimoire open, desperate. "There has to be something..."

"We must try again," Aldric urged. "Something to bind him. Even if it only buys time."

Thomelin's eyes scanned the runes, now shifting before his gaze. He recognized a sequence and symbol in the grimoire. It was similar to one from the old book he read years ago and using some of these new symbols maybe he could reverse or trap him.

He dropped to one knee and began drawing fresh symbols in the ground, this time not with chalk but with the very blackened soil itself. His voice shook, uncertain but urgent, as he began to recite.

Corwin crouched beside him, sword in hand, watching the trembling horizon for signs of movement. Garran stood with his back to the others, guarding the half-collapsed threshold that now looked out onto a pulsing black plain instead of the hill they'd ridden up.

As Thomelin chanted, the air shimmered. Not with light, but with distortion: as though the air itself was trying to pull away from what was happening.

"These symbols... they're reacting," Thomelin muttered. "He let us have this book. But not everything in it serves him and he thinks us too foolish."

Another crack split the earth. Something beneath it groaned.

"You mimic my words like children reciting hymns," Caelomin said, closer now. *"You do not understand what they summon. Your kind never did."*

The room pulsed with invisible pressure. One of the candles reignited on its own with a burst of cold blue flame.

Thomelin pushed on, louder now, more sure. He traced the final sigil and shouted the last word.

The ground split open at the circle's center, and a column of black fire erupted: not heat, but cold, burning into their vision. A shape flickered in it: wings, eyes, shifting geometry that defied description.

Corwin crossed the threshold to help Thomelin.

"Keep going," Corwin said. *"Whatever this is, it's working."*

"I'm not sure how this will work, it may not trap him fully," Thomelin replied, sweating now. "Not enough to seal him again. But it's... it's interfering. Confusing him. It may hold for a moment."

"Then we use it," Aldric barked. "If it buys us one breath, we take it."

The distorted space at the center twisted violently. Caelomin's form coalesced within: humanoid, angelic, blinding. His true self pushed through the veil now, wings of light wrapped in language and decay.

"You defy me with borrowed words and stolen lines," Caelomin hissed.

Thomelin clutched the book tighter, despite its biting heat. "Then maybe next time, don't write your traps into your own scripture."

The unnatural light flared again. The binding symbols cracked and began to unravel.

"He's breaking it!" one shouted.

Corwin raised his sword, eyes locking with Garran's. They knew what must come next.

And behind them, the sky began to bleed.

The sky wept blood.

It ran in slow, celestial sheets across the cracks above them: red not like wine or gore, but like molten memory. It slid along the edges of the illusory tower, staining the bones of its deceit. The ritual ground trembled. The horizon (if it could still be called that) folded in on itself, drawing closer with each heartbeat.

The knights no longer stood in a room. The boundaries of the world had peeled back to reveal the altar beneath it. Trees of ash writhed in the distance, their bark split with crying mouths. The soil pulsed like a dying heart beneath their boots.

Caelomin rose higher from the rift, vast and sovereign like a forgotten king clawing his way out a shattered tomb to reclaim his throne from ruin, his wings unfurled in broken majesty, once radiant spilling holy light now darkening to a corrupted furious blood red glow that stained the air like a curse.

He was what angels become when left to fester in silence and grief until faith sours into wrath, his face shifting between seraphic beauty and a nightmare crowned in smoke and judgement.

"There is no salvation, no mercy, your heaven remains silent, no light but mines" Caelomin thundered. "The age of Caelomin dawns, Repent! Before I set your world to flame"

Thomelin's hands trembled over the burning grimoire. "We need more time," he said, half to himself. "I can improvise the pattern: stack a second ring, bleed the current one into it. It won't hold him... but it might trap his voice. Confuse him longer."

"How long?" Corwin asked.

"Long enough. Maybe. You can escape. I know I must stay in the circle till its complete but I need someone else."

There was no need to explain. They all understood. The circle demanded blood to hold, the weight of sacrifice hung in the air, heavy and holy and each man knew one of them would have to stand in the circle with Thomelin never to leave, that would be the price.

Aldric stepped forward without hesitation. His expression was calm, too calm. The others didn't stop him. They knew better. He had carried this burden longer than any of them.

"Thomelin, what do I need to do?"

Thomelin looked up, reluctant, grief flashing through his eyes. "Step inside the first circle. When I say the words, place your hand on the broken glyph and say your name. That will anchor the transition. But..."

"There's no 'but,'" Aldric said. "Do it."

Corwin moved closer. "You don't have to..."

Aldric turned. His eyes met Corwin's, soft with unspoken memory. "I do."

Behind them, Caelomin reeled in his own rage. The partial ritual had wounded him: not in the way mortals bleed, but in how a god recoils when reminded it is not whole. His form shimmered, distorted. Eyes blinked open along his wings. Some cried. Some watched.

Thomelin began again. Faster this time. The new ring carved itself through the loose earth as his voice called forth impossible shapes. Lines glowed. The soil ignited: not with fire, but with purpose.

Aldric stepped into the ring. He looked impossibly small there.

The moment Thomelin spoke the final word, the entire landscape convulsed. A vortex of black sound tore through the world, swallowing the color from the air. Caelomin howled: not from pain, but fury. His form bent sideways, reality buckling beneath him.

"Say it!" Thomelin shouted.

Aldric stood tall. His voice did not shake. "I am Aldric of Veyne. I offer my name to bind the light."

The ground exploded.

Light (if it could be called that) rushed outward in a scream. Caelomin's form was dragged back, his voice fracturing into ten thousand discordant echoes. The sigils spun like shields of salt and fire, creating a cage not of matter, but of memory, symbol, and belief.

The ritual flared, then collapsed.

The circle shattered, and Aldric and Thomelin with it. There was no scream, no sound. Just a pulse, a breath, a moment of unbeing. Then silence.

Caelomin vanished nut the earth remained defiled, a scorched black wound, no grass would grow there no prayer would reach it, Of Aldric and Thomelin there was no trace, they were simply gone.

Garran was on his knees. Corwin knelt beside him, gripping his shoulder, the grimoire now a pile of silent ash.

For a time, no one spoke.

Then the sky began to brighten: not with sun, but with grey. The illusion was gone. The false tower gone. They stood on desecrated land, black and twisted. Nothing remained of the tower. Only ruin, and silence, and the weight of what they had almost freed.

Corwin stared at the scorched earth where Aldric and Thomelin once stood. "They did it, but Aldric and Thomelin…are they…."

Garran nodded numbly. "they gave their lifes to stop that thing to save us and maybe everyone beyond this place, we owe them more than dying here beside them. we need to leave While we still can "

Corwin bent low, lifting Aldric's scorched iron cross and Thomelin's sword, the metal blackened and warped as though it had tasted fire itself. He said nothing only tightening his grip on both relics as if holding the men who once wielded them.

Corwin helped Garran limp towards the horizon, dawn was breaking pale and colourless over the battlefield. Before they crossed the ridge Corwin tuned one last time to the place Aldric and Thomelin had stood, his lips parted but no prayer came only a raw hallow grief.

Then it came, a sound beneath the churned soil, deep and terrible, a scream that seemed to claw its way toward the surface. It rose for a heartbeat vast and inhuman…then it stopped.

Complete silence followed, They turned and walked on without looking back.

16

The Silence-Broken Aegis

Corwin returned home in the grey hours before dawn. Mud clung to his boots like a second skin. His cloak was torn, crusted with blood that was not all his own. He didn't remember the journey down from the blighted hilltop. He only remembered Garran walking beside him, neither of them speaking, the wind wailing like a widow in mourning.

Adelyne opened the door before he knocked.

She didn't speak. She just looked at him (his face pale, his eyes sunken) and stepped aside. He stepped inside and dropped to his knees, burying his face in her stomach. Her fingers found his hair. He stayed there a long time, trembling like a man waking from a nightmare he still half-believed.

He never told her the truth.

In the days that followed, Corwin tried to live. The land remembered the war, and so did his bones. He worked the fields. He mended broken fences. He built a home with hands that had broken bones and drawn steel. He smiled when his daughter was born and wept quietly when his son first reached for his hand.

But every night, he woke with a start.

In dreams, the tower still stood. The tower that never was. He heard Aldric's voice, steady and brave. He saw Thomelin's hands shaking over the grimoire. He heard Caelomin laughing from behind thin stone, promising the end of all things.

He told no one. Not even Adelyne.

Instead, he read. He researched. He travelled to old churches and monasteries under other pretenses. He memorized the names of exorcists and heretics, saints and scholars. In secret, he built a room beneath their house filled with books he never let the children see.

Years passed. The world moved on. The war faded from memory, and peace settled over the kingdom like fresh snow. Garran disappeared into the west, vowing to bury himself where the wind would forget his name. Corwin heard nothing for years.

He aged. But not too much. Still strong in his late forties. Still quiet, still watchful. Still waiting.

One morning, the sky threatened snow.

Corwin walked alone through the village. He carried a small bundle wrapped in cloth and twine. The chapel door creaked open as he entered. No one else was there. He walked behind it to the graveyard.

Two stones stood there. Simple. Unmarked but for a cross carved into each. He knelt before them, the cloth bundle cradled in his calloused hands.

He opened it carefully.

Inside: a scrap of white cloth, now yellowed by time (the last piece of the ribbon Adelyne had given him so long ago).

And a rusted shard of an old knight's cross, broken clean in two.

He laid them down gently, one on each grave.

"Thank you," he whispered. His voice cracked, rough with years of silence. "For giving me the years you never had."

The wind picked up. Snowflakes spun in slow, lazy spirals through the grey.

He stood, heart heavy but steady. He turned from the graves and walked down the village's main road, snow beginning to gather in the seams of his cloak.

That's when he heard it.

A shout. Not far ahead.

Rounding the corner, Corwin saw them: five or six men, red-faced and jeering, surrounding a smaller, ragged figure pressed against a wall. The victim (young, pale, maybe a beggar) had his hands up, pleading.

Corwin's boots crunched on the frost-hardened road as he approached. One of the thugs turned.

"Go on, old man," the brute barked. "This ain't your..."

"Always the big tough men, aren't you?" Corwin said quietly, cutting him off.

His voice wasn't loud. It didn't need to be. There was steel in it.

"Always think you're the great terror, the big baddie everyone's too scared to face. I've seen worse crawling through the dark." He stepped forward, eyes unblinking. "And I'm not going to let it happen again."

The thugs paused. The leader's lip curled.

Corwin didn't blink.

Something in his gaze (a weight, an echo of a world beyond this one) made the gang back down. One muttered something under his breath. The others followed, slipping away down the road like smoke before flame.

Corwin stepped up to the young man, helped him to his feet.

"You're safe," he said softly. "Go."

The young man stammered thanks, then ran.

Corwin sighed, his breath rising in a mist.

And then he felt it.

A presence. Behind him.

He turned slowly.

A figure stood at the far edge of the square.

Heavy cloak. Grey in the snow. A scar across the brow. Broad shoulders.

Garran.

Alive. Older. Haunted.

Corwin stared. For a long moment, neither spoke.

Then Garran stepped forward, boots crunching in time with the falling snow.

"I thought I'd find you here," Garran said quietly.

Corwin's breath caught.

And before he could speak, Garran finished:

"He's back."

The snow fell heavier around them.

Garran didn't say how he knew. He didn't need to. The look in his eyes was enough.

They stood for a time in silence, snow curling between them, the cold forgotten. Corwin studied Garran: the scarred brow, the rigid set of his jaw, the cloak still dusted with travel and frost. Time had not softened him. If anything, it had carved him deeper.

"Come inside," Corwin said.

They crossed the threshold of Corwin's home, boots heavy with slush. The fire was low. Adelyne had long since gone to bed. Nothing was said as Corwin led Garran through the quiet house. Past the hearth, past the small room where his children slept.

He opened the hidden door.

It was cleverly built into the floor beneath the kitchen. Just a warped old trapdoor to any outsider. But beneath it...

Garran descended slowly, step by step, eyes narrowing as they adjusted to the flickering lamplight below. The room was cramped, its walls stacked with ancient texts, scrolls, and relics. Shelves overflowed with fragments of bone, dried flowers, cracked icons, and soot-darkened pages inked in Latin, Hebrew, tongues older still.

Corwin lit the main lantern and let it glow.

Garran let out a low breath. "You've been busy."

"For years," Corwin said. "I didn't know what I was looking for. But I knew I had to be ready."

Garran's gaze hardened, his voice a rough whisper. "Aye... I've been busy too. I've walked through places no knight should walk. Sat in graveyards where the dead still whispered. Shared fires with men who serve nothing but rot and madness. Listened to cults pray to things older than our God, just to hear their lies and find a shard of truth."

He pulled a small bundle from his pack, wrapped in stained cloth, the twine frayed to threads. When he unwrapped it, a crude charm lay in his palm, a figure kneeling, head bowed, worn smooth by time and many desperate hands. Garran held it like it was the last scrap of faith he owned.

"An old witch in the east gave me this," he said quietly. "Swore it would guard the soul against things not born of this world. Maybe it's madness... but after what we saw, I'll take madness over ignorance."

Corwin nodded and placed the charm gently beside a bowl of salt and dried sprigs of heather.

"There's power in belief," he said. "Even madness has its shape."

The two men sat in silence, surrounded by centuries of forgotten truths.

When they finally climbed back upstairs, the fire had nearly gone out. The house was still.

Corwin opened the door, letting in the night air. They stood on the porch, side by side, watching the snow drift down in slow, steady spirals.

Neither spoke of what would come next.

There was nothing to say.

Above them, clouds gathered, grey and slow. This soil they stood on now had never known the slaughter they'd left behind in the fields of death and in their hearts, they knew they would have to walk those grounds again.

Corwin closed his eyes. The dread began to build again, creeping like ice through his veins. And then carried faintly on the wind, came a sound that made his blood run colder still, a low, dark laugh, far away yet meant for him to hear.

He opened his eyes.

"For Aldric," Corwin murmured.

"And Thomelin," Garran added.

The snow fell heavier around them burying the world beneath white silence., smothering all sound, all warmth, In the stillness, Corwin's breath catches sharply in his throat as he stares into the gathering darkness, feeling it again, that ancient presence, vast and relentless, hungering now for vengeance.

Corwins gaze drifted downward, to his children's toys lying half-buried beneath the snow, small and innocent against the encroaching darkness. Garran places a firm, heavy hand on his shoulder.

"You feel it too," Garran said, quiet and grim.

Corwin nodded slowly, voice tight with resolve. "It won't stop. Not until everything we love is ash. This time, we have to end it…forever."

The snow deepened around their feet, Corwin knew the truth, the thing they buried was awake now, and it was coming for them all.

A Note to the Reader

Authors run on caffeine and reviews.

I'm nearly out of both.

Help a writer out. Leave a few words on Amazon before the shadows claim me.

About the author

David Adams is a Scottish writer of dark fiction, blending horror, theology, and myth into atmospheric tales of dread and survival. When not writing, he's likely somewhere cold, caffeinated, and planning his next nightmare.

Printed in Dunstable, United Kingdom